The Unromantic Love Birds

And other short stories about love and marriages

'Dipo Toby Alakija

ISBN: 978 - 978- 49874-5-5
ISBN: 978-49847-5-7

Printed in United States

First published in2012 and republished in 2016 by

CALVARY ROCK RESOURCES

19, Ajina Street, Ikenne Remo,
Ogun State,
Nigeria.

36, Thomson road
Gorton
Manchester
M18 7QQ
United Kingdom

270 Madison Avenue
Suite 1500, New York, NY 10016
United States

www.calvaryrock.org

Dedication

This book is dedicated to my uncle, Pastor Ope Odesanya whose wealth of experience in marriage has tremendous impact in my life and in the major story.

MIXED PASSION

ONE

'... The Lord told me that the man that would marry you is a hard drinker and a fornicator,' the pastor told Ann who had previously gone to him for counseling. She had been praying for a husband since she came to Nigeria from the United States.

'How can God tell you a thing like that, pastor?' Ann asked, looking puzzled. 'I mean I could have picked a man like that in the States if I had wanted to. You know, the country is so full of them.'

The pastor was a shrewd looking and middle aged man with a reputation of a dynamic minister of the full gospel. 'Well,' he sa d, 'you probably don't understand. The man is still in the world. You're going to meet him soon because you have a duty to minister to his soul.'

Ann viewed the whole situation with a more confused expression. She was well tutored and cultured in Christian ethics. She has a doctoral degree in Applied Mathematics from one of the most prestigious Universities... and she had a good job in US before she was forced to come to Nigeria, her father's home country to take the post of a lecturer at the Lagos State University. She had left virtually every good thing she could think of in America because many preachers seemed to have the same word for her that her would-be husband was in Nigeria. She had been told that God has a special assignment for her and her would-be husband in Africa. She was told if she wanted to obey God, she has to come to Nigeria. In obedience to what God seemed to be telling her through the ministers, she came to the country in spite of the discomfort. The first thing she did when she got to the country was to get identified with a gospel Church where she was instantly recognized as a strong and seasoned Christian. There was a prophecy that she was going to be a vessel of honour in the hands of God. So she was given an opportunity to minister in the Word of God one Sunday. Soon after that, the pastor made her one of the Bible teachers in the Church. She began to do all she could do in the Church with the little time she could afford, fasting and praying that God would make available the man He had ordained to be her husband.

It was at the end of one Sunday service that the pastor called and informed Ann that her husband to be would soon surface and that he was a drinker and a fornicator.

'These are the two things I hate most in a man!' Ann said in frustration. 'How could God bring me all the way from America to be married to a drinker and a fornicator? I really find it hard to believe this.'

The pastor sighed. 'Sometimes it takes determination to do the will of God. As a matter of fact, the will of God seems so hard for you because of the nature of the work of God you have to do with the man. Besides, we were all lost in our sins before coming to Christ. You were in the mud when God sent someone to pick you up, remember.'

Ann could see his point. She would not forget how the Lord saved her when she was lost in the company of sinful friends when she newly got admitted for her first degree in the University. Her friends influenced her to be involved in sexual immoralities until a lady told her about Jesus. Though she did not do anything about what she was told for a long time but, when Jesus came to her in the dream in the form of an old man and told her she was heading to hell, she decided to hand over her life to Him.

'The same thing is with this man,' the pastor said, not conscious of her deep thoughts. 'Christ is all he needs before he becomes a perfect man for you. What I think you should do is to pray to God to bring the man across your way. How He would do that is not for us to be worried about.'

Months later, the church organized a four days crusade and invited a famous preacher as the guest speaker. A lot of people were invited into the Church. The beginning of the crusade was so uplifting that it attracted more people into the Church. Before the end of the crusade, the number of people attending the Church had increased. Ann who was among the Sunday school teachers that took the new convert class was faced with so many newcomers. The class was spilt into two so that Ann and one other teacher would find it convenient to teach and follow up the students as was the normal practice in the Church.

Ann had three married couple, five ladies and four gentlemen in her class. She got all the addresses of her students at the end of the Sunday school and promised to pay each of them a visit before the following Sunday.

'I want you to prepare me a very local food,' she joked. Her students who were aware that she grew up and schooled in America through the way she spoke smiled at her.

'Do you know how to eat Eba?' a woman called Sola asked.

'Yes!' she replied quickly.

'Really?' another of her student called Rex asked, looking and smiling at her.

Ann smiled back at the students. 'It's okay,' she said. 'You con't have to border yourself about that. I'm just joking but I know the food is made of heavy stuff - cassava or something. Am I right?'

'Yes, ma,' Sola said.

'You don't have to visit me if you won't eat Eba,' Rex insisted. He seemed to be the most vocal among the students. He was fond of saying something even if he really did not have anything to say.

Somehow, Ann felt she needed to visit him before others. He sounded like a sanguine type of person. From her experience, people in that category of temperament were usually noisy and indiscipline. To ensure that he remained a Christian, she would expose him to the word of God. 'You're brother...?' she asked, smiling at him.

'Rex Famida,' he said.

'You'll be my first host,' she said. 'I'll surprise you. I'll not only eat Eba, I'll also eat rats.'

All the students laughed.

'What rat?' another student called Femi asked. 'We don't eat rats in Nigeria!'

'What do you mean?' Ann asked, somewhat surprised. 'I've eaten it before. A church member gave it to me few weeks ago.'

'You probably ate bush rat,' Rex said, laughing with others.

'Bush and house rats don't make any difference, do they?' Ann asked, looking more confused.

Her confusion made the rest laughed the more.

'In America,' she said, 'we don't eat rat at all. I had to pray for grace of God before I coulc eat the rat because I don't want to disappoint the people that gave it to me.

The discussion after Sunday school was a little delightful. The students became more attracted to Ann. She was so lovely and loving that every student was eager to host her at his or her homes.

Ann tried hard to fulfill the promise she made to her students despite her tight schedule as a lecturer. It was in the evening of each day of the week, apart from the days for prayer meetings and bible studies that she managed to drive round their homes, first visiting the couples. She later visited the people that seemed to be in need with gifts of food and other items. Contrary to what she planned, Rex was the last person she was able to visit before the next worship service. She got to his house at the unexpected hour. Her apartment was really

4

far from where he lived but, as it was common in Lagos metropolis, she was held up in traffic jams. She was able to trace his address at around nine at night.

Rex lived in an estate that was owned by a very big oil company in Nigeria. The whole area was beautiful and impressive looking.

Ann parked her lovely car in front of one of flats, which the guessed was Rex's and got down, heading for the entrance. She strode towards the flat and rang the doorbell. After waiting for a long time, a lady came to open the door.

The appearance of the lady was an eyesore to Ann. She wore only a very transparent cloth, which revealed every part of her naked body. Her face was snared with make-up. Her looks and gestures showed she was slightly drunk.

Ann hoped that Rex didn't live with a lady like that. No man would stay with such a lady without being seduced even if he didn't intended to make love to her.

'Hello,' the lady said, looking tipsy.

'Good evening,' Ann said politely. 'I'm ... em looking for Brother Rex Famida.'

The lady noted she did not pronounce the second name correctly. She frowned at her, making her thought she had missed the flat. Ann hoped she had missed his flat anyway.

'You're not from this country?' the lady asked.

'Actually, I'm a Nigerian,' Ann said, smiling at her. 'But I grew up in US.'

'I see,' she said. 'What do you want from Rex?'

'He's... em... just one of our church members,' Ann said gently.

'I see,' she said. Ann expected her to point to his flat or at least let her in but she didn't. She simply called, 'Rex!'

There was a soft answer form within.

'Tidy yourself up,' the lady said. 'You've got a decent lady here as a visitor.'

Ann was not yet surprised until she saw Rex on the couch in the lavishly furnished sitting room, wrapped in long towel, looking as tipsy as the lady. There were three empty bottles of beer on the floor.

She didn't need to make any investigation before she knew that Rex and the lady had been messing around. She hid her surprise with a pleasant smile and said, 'hello, brother Rex.'

Rex was so embarrassed that he became sober at once. He stood up immediately and hurried inside with shame, mumbling to be spared some minutes.

Ann did not know whether to share her opinion about him by addressing the issue of sin or find another time to tell him since it was getting late already.

Rex was in the room with the lady who was on the bed, expecting him to do away with Ann and join her on the bed.

Rex felt like a hypocrite. He did not know how to make up for the perverted life Ann just discovered about him. He suddenly hated his life and the sexually promiscuous lady he was hanging around with. He told the lady, 'Funmi, get dressed. You have to leave my house now.'

'What did you say, Rex?' she asked, looking surprised.

'You heard me right. I said leave,' he said curtly. 'And I mean now!'

'You want me to leave because of that girl?' she asked. 'Is she your latest girlfriend?'

'If you mean well for both of us, leave now!' He went to take some money in the wardrobe and stretched it to her. 'Take that for a taxi.'

'What do you take me for? A whore?' she asked, glaring at him.

'You're not a whore. Just leave, please.'

'What if I say it's too late for me to go anywhere?'

'It's not late. It's just twenty minutes after nine. You can get a taxi even by eleven p.m.'

'What if I say I won't go?'

'I will simply throw you out!' he growled, irritated. He did not even know why he should persuade her to leave his house in the first place. After all, she was just his bed partner and nothing more. Besides, the unexpected presence of Ann in his house really demanded he should take that step if he wanted to encourage her to visit him. He has developed a deep respect for the lady. Merely making friends with her alone was a great honour. He was not ready sacrifice the friendship for anything or anyone.

The lady went to put her cloths which she dropped beside the bed before making love. When she was fully dressed, she went to look at him straight in the eyes. 'You're a beast. You're not fit to be a man. I could send hired killers to waste your miserable life but I won't do that because I know fully well that you'll soon come back to your senses. You'll come soon to me when you need me.'

Rex waved the money to her, 'you still need this?'

She snatched the money from him. He almost laughed. He knew that was all that could calm her down.

'I wish you go right straight to blazes,' she said.

He pointed at the door. 'Out.'

She went out and slammed the door. She went pass Ann who was still standing, wondering what was going on.

'Oh, sister...' Ann attempted. But she didn't listen to her. She hurried away angrily.

Rex came out some minutes later, wearing a T-shirt and a pair of trousers. He looked so ashamed that he could not look at her face.

'Who is that lady?' Ann asked gently, trying to help him overcome his embarrassment.

He hesitated for a long time before he said, 'I'm afraid you're asking about the atrocity you just discovered about me.'

'I suppose you work in an oil company?'

He nodded.

'What's your position in the place?'

'I'm an engineer.'

'Do you mind if you tell me how old you are?'

'I'm thirty-one,' he replied, still unable to look at her face. 'Won't you sit down?' he asked, waving her to a couch with apparent discomfort.

'Thank you,' she said, taking her seat. He sat opposite her, looking away. She was moved by his humility, modesty and feelings of guilt. Even though she was hopping to leave the house soonest, she decided to address the issue of sin right away instead of waiting till another day. 'Do you plan to marry the lady?'

He shook his head slowly.

'Why not?'

'I know she is not the lady God wants me to marry.'

'How do you know that?' she asked almost jocularly though she was getting uncomfortable with his feeling of guilt.

'I just know.'

'You expect God to give you a responsible woman to marry, isn't it?'

'Naturally, everybody would like a responsible person as a spouse.'

She smiled, feeling the need to address the issue of sin and not his conduct. 'At least, you're sincere and you feel embarrassed that I found the lady with you.' There was a brief silence before she said, 'there's this question that keeps ringing in my mind since I got here. Why don't you get married instead of messing around with a lady? With your status in this country and at your age, I expect you to have gotten married.' She paused. 'Am I intruding into your personal life or something?'

7

Rex glanced at her. 'Oh no,' he said quickly. 'I love your interest in my affairs. In fact I give you the right to inquire about anything about my life. After all you are my Bible teacher and a.... friend, aren': you?'

'If you want it so, let it be so.'

He smiled for the first time and said, 'thank you.'

'I thank you too for giving me that liberty and privilege,' she said.

'You're so humble, Doctor Ann. You consider it a privilege that a sinner like me is taken as your friend.'

Ann found it strange that they both considered each other humble. 'Call me Sister Ann, please, and believe that we are all nothing without the grace of God.'

'I'm learning,' he said quietly.

'If you really want to learn, tell me sincerely what actually is wrong with your life. I want to see how to address the issue of sin and possibly assist you with prayers.'

'Really,' he said, 'I would have been a good Christian if not that I.... I have relationships with different ladies and I.... em drink. Those are my two major problems.'

'Either of them is enough to get you to hell,' she said. 'Do you want to go to hell?'

'No sane person would like to go to hell.'

'If you don't want to go the place, why committing sins? Perhaps the question I should have asked is how real is hell and heaven to you?'

He looked thoughtful. 'I'm not sure how real it is.'

'That explains why you feel no qualms about committing sins.' She paused briefly before she said, 'can you get your Bible and read a passage with me?'

He went to get the Bible while she brought out a small one from her handbag.

'I would like to share with you a portion in the Bible that explains the condition of someone that takes alcoholic drinks. Let me tell you something mysterious about Samson whom I believe you must have heard about. Before he was born, the angel of God appeared to his mother to tell her about the birth of Samson who God planned to use to deliver the people of Israel from the hands of the philistines. The angel spoke to his mother in Judges chapter 3 verses 3 to 5 which say, "And the angel of the LORD appeared unto the woman, and said unto her, Behold now, thou art barren, and bearest not: but thou shalt conceive, and bear a son.

'"Now therefore beware, I pray thee, and drink not wine nor strong drink, and eat not any unclean thing:

'"For, lo, thou shalt conceive, and bear a son; and no razor shall come on his head: for the child shall be a Nazarite unto God from the womb: and he shall begin to deliver Israel out of the hand of the Philistines."'

She looked at him after she finished reading and went on, 'Now, when you study the life history of Samson, you'll discover that it was two things that the enemies used to get him down. First, they used a woman whom he could not do without. Then the woman gave him some wine, which eventually caused him to reveal the secret of his strength. That was what led to his untimely death.

'All Christians are supposed to be Nazarites because Jesus, our role model is of Nazareth. If a Christian takes alcoholic drinks, it means he is either spiritually dead or dying or he is yet to become a Christian. Christians are filled with the Spirit of God and not with wine so that they can deliver the people from the devil, their enemies just as Samson was to deliver the people of Israel from the Philistines.

'Take a look at the passage in Proverbs chapter 20 verse 1, which says: "Wine is a mocker, strong drink is raging: and whosoever is deceived thereby is not wise." Do you see the point? Exactly what that passage says is what happened to Samson in the book of Judges Chapter 16. What happened in the passage was that after Samson revealed the secrets of his strength to the woman called Delilah through the influence of the wine she gave to him, his head was shaved and brought before his enemies. Hear what the Bible says in verse 23 of that Chapter: "Then the lords of the Philistines gathered them together for to offer a great sacrifice unto Dagon their god, and to rejoice: for they said, our god hath delivered Samson our enemy into our hand."

'You see how Samson subjected himself into ridicule just because he failed to abstain from taking alcoholic drinks.

'I believe God gave Samson strength to destroy the Philistines just to protect His name which the enemies have defiled. If not, he would not get the strength to destroy the enemies of God's people.

'Similarly, so many Christians find themselves in the position of Samson when they take wine. They start saying and thinking all sorts of things which sometimes defile the name of the Lord. They get involved in unholy affairs or relationships. You know, one thing will lead to another. What do you expect to happen if you drink beer like sinners, get involved with a lady that is ready lure you to bed? It becomes a light thing to sin against God just like the people of the world. The power of the Holy Spirit will go from the life of that person just as Samson's strength disappeared. Once the power of the Holy Spirit is gone, that person is vulnerable to attacks of the devil. Besides, if that person is identified with Christ, the name of the Lord would be dragged in the mud. The devil can come around and begin to kick him like football. He would disgrace him and turn him into a meat or … or an object of mockery just as the Philistines did to Samson by plucking out his eyes. Surely, you wouldn't like to risk ending up like that, would you?'

Rex shook his head slowly. He was really moved by what she was saying.

'The problem of drinking can be overcome,' she said in a more gentle voice, 'if you make up your mind to stop drinking and the problem of fornication can be solved with the passage in I Corinthians 7:9 which says, "But if they cannot contain, let them marry for it is better to marry than to burn." That simply means that if you cannot keep yourself from having affairs with ladies, it is better for you to marry a lady than to continue in fornication and then end up in hell.' She paused for a long time, looking at his sober face. 'I hope all I've said make sense to you?'

'It makes a lot of sense so me,' he said quietly.

'If it makes sense, then let's pray.' She prayed for sometimes before she decided to go.

'Wait a minute, Sister Ann,' Rex said, going to his room. 'I have something for you.' He took an envelope on his reading table, opened his wardrobe and brought out some money. He put as much money as he could afford inside it and closed it. It was so bulky that it couldn't close very well. He folded it together and took it to Ann who was already on her feet.

He handed the envelope to her away.

'Oh, no, no, I don't need it. I'm sorry.'

Rex suddenly looked sad.

'You're supposed to prepare Eba for me,' Ann said, trying to cheer him up. 'That was the deal, isn't it? Eba with bush rat is what I expect you to offer me, not money.' She paused to look at his face. He was silent, looking so sorrowful that she wondered if she had said anything wrong. 'Guess what! I'll eat any rat meat if you can cook it for me when next I come!'

He didn't laugh as she expected. He said, 'I'll take it that you reject the money because I'm a sinner - a terrible sinner.'

'Oh, no, brother Rex,' she said quickly. 'Don't interpret it that way.

10

As far as I'm concerned and as far as I believe God is concerned, you have not done anything because God have forgiven you.'

'If so,' he said,' you can convince me by taking his money from me as a friend.'

She hesitated for a long time, not knowing what so do. Although she didn't really find anything wrong in taking the money from him but she just did not like the idea.

'By taking money, Sister Ann,' he said, 'you're giving joy. Please, take it if you want me to be happy.'

'Alright,' she said with a sigh, 'if you insist.' She took the money. She studied at him. 'Thanks,' she said. 'Are you happy now?'

He nodded vigorously, smiling.

'I brought roasted meat for you just as I gave to other Sunday school students in my class. It's in my car,' she said. 'Would you be happy to take it from me?'

He looked so delighted that she felt greater joy within her. 'Wao!' he said, 'I'm really going to have a nice time doing justice to it.'

She laughed as they went to the car together.

She gave him the roasted meat. He quickly took a bite to show her he appropriate it. 'It tastes like bush rat,' he said. 'I love it…'

'It's not bush rat,' she said. 'It's a big rat I killed in my house.'

'What?' He pretended to be shocked.

She burst into laughter that lasted some minutes. 'Just kidding,' she said when she got over her laughter.

Again, he pretended to be relieved.

'See you on Sunday,' she said, sitting behind the wheel. She started the car and drove away. He waved to her before he went back to his flat, feeling very delighted.

TWO

Ann got home and threw herself heavily on the couch in her two bedrooms flat. The flat was reasonably well furnished with mostly things she brought from US.

She opened her hand bag to take the envelop Rex had given her. She only observed that the envelope was bulky but she never had any idea how much was inside. She opened it. To her surprise, she discovered that the amount was as much as half of her monthly salary.

'W-what....' She muttered to herself. 'Oh, my God!' She knew she had to tell the pastor about this.

The following Sunday, Rex was in the church. During the Sunday school, Ann greeted all her students warmly and remarked on each of them.

'Brother Rex was very generous to me,' she said. 'Really, I got more than I bargained for from all my hosts. May God bless you all of you. I'll do my best to visit the rest of you this week.'

The students that were visited too thanked her for the presents she gave them.

'I enjoyed the rat,' Rex said cheerfully.

The rest laughed.

'Next time I visit you,' Ann said, ' I might get you an antelope or elephant.'

'Can we take that as a promise?' Rex asked jocularly.

'I'm just joking!' Ann said, laughing with others. 'Where in the world do you expect me to get the animals?'

'We have them roaming around the forest,' one of the female students said.

'All right, we'll go and look for them together just the two of us!'

The students laughed again. The lively discussion led them into prayers before they began the Sunday school.

At the end of the Church service, Ann went to see the pastor in the office.

'Something unusual is happening, pastor,' she told him. 'There's one of my students called Brother Rex Famida in the Sunday school. He was one of the students I visited this week-end and... I got to his

12

house late around nine p.m. I was held up in a traffic jam. Well, I'm not sure if I should tell you this.'

'Tell me only what you feel I should know.'

'Well ... em ... I met a lady with him whom he confessed he was having an affair with. Both of them were a little drunk. He sent the lady away when I got there. I tried to talk to the lady but she was too angry to listen to me... I shared the word of God with brother Rex. What really surprised me was the amount of money he gave me.'

'He gave you some money?' the pastor asked.

'Well-yes. I'm sorry,' Ann said quickly. 'I tried to reject it but he told me he took it that I rejected the money because he's a terrible sinner.'

'I see,' the pastor said thoughtfully.

'The reason I feel I should tell you is because I didn't expect the money to be so much. It was when I got home that I opened the envelope,' she sounded awkward as she opened her bag to bring out the money.

'On no, Sister Ann,' the pastor said quickly.

She paused to look at him.

'It's okay. I don't think it's wrong for you so take the money from him really. What I was thinking is the discussion we had together few months ago. You remember what I said during the discussion.'

'Yes, sir,' she said. 'You said the Lord told you that the man He has for me is a hard drinker and a fornicator.'

'I also said, if you remember very well, that he would soon surface.'

She looked thoughtful for a while. She could recall it vividly. She remembered Rex telling her the problem he has with women. She could almost hear him saying, "Really, I would have been a good Christian if not that I ... have relationship with different ladies and I ... drink. Those are my two problems..." She wondered if he was really the man God planned to be her husband. Though with what has happened so far and with what he had told her about himself, he might be the man she had been praying for. 'No,' she argued within herself. It was found it hard to imagine it.

'I don't want you to conclude yet,' the pastor said, jerking Ann out of her thoughts, 'but I want you to pray about it and continue to follow up the brother until he is delivered from the bondage of sins. At least God wants him to be among His children, if not to be your future husband.'

She looked reluctant. 'I wish you could give some else the assignment, sir.'

13

The pastor smiled. 'You're afraid he may turn out to be the man?'

'No, sir,' she replied quickly. 'I don't want undue attachment that…, you know.'

'I don't see your point, sister Ann.' The pastor was obviously laughing at her.

'It can affect many things.'

'Even if there is someone else that can follow him up, I won't assign anyone else with that job. He's your responsibility. For one, he's your student in the Sunday school and your child in the Lord. Secondly, I'm not the one that gives you the assignment. God did. He expects you to at least feed him until he's matured. You can tell God you cannot follow the soul he has placed in your care. You can give him your reason. He may understand your reason. I don't.'

'Okay,' Ann said in resignation. 'I'll do the best I can to reach him.'

'Good,' the pastor said cheerfully. 'And don't forget to pray for him, for yourself and the church.'

Since the pastor made Ann to see that Rex's spiritual grow was partly her responsibility, she began to pay close attention to him. Then the thought that it was possible that God intended him to be her husband in future began to haunt her like a spirit. Even though she was a naturally pleasant and docile lady, she became upset constantly, especially each time the thought of him crossed her mind. Really, Rex was a man many ladies would love to marry. He was good looking, modest, sincere and generous. But what she knew about him was devastating. In fact, the negative sides of him made her not to pay any regard to his good virtues. On the whole, she could make herself to love or despise him. She chose not to despise him because she knew God did not expect that attitude from her even toward any human being like herself. Because she did not want to despise him, she paid closer attention to his virtues and that made her to begin to love him as days went by.

She tried as much to keep in touch with all Sunday school students either by calling them on the phone or going to see them. Rex was no exception.

Rex took every opportunity he had to prove that he was a man of perfect virtues in spite of the negative aspect of him. He always stocked some money into her hand bag each time she came to visit him. She complained to him the first time she discovered it, saying him on the phone, 'I wish you don't have to play such game with me.'

He repeated it again. Then she decided she would either leave her bag in the car or hold it through out the time she was sharing the word of God with him at home. When he noticed her determination not to take anything from him, he said quietly, 'I can see that you have made up your mind never to take anything from the miserable sinner you are trying to get out of the mud.' He shrugged as he added in a quiet voice as if he pitied himself, 'the only way I feel I could show that I appreciate your spiritual contribution into my life is to sow into your life. By taking the money, you're actually helping me.'

The way he said it moved her. 'Alright,' she said softly. 'I'll take whatever you give me but I must warn you that it doesn't actually encourage me to come here.'

'I can always come to your place.'

'You know it would be a waste of time trying to reach me at home,' she said. 'Let's reach a compromise. If you want to encourage me to visit and share the word of God with you, there should be no game.'

'I'm not trying to play games with you. You know that.'

'That's not what I mean.'

'That's what you just said.'

'Let me try to explain it this way,' she said. 'It's wrong to take anything from you.'

'Why not?' he asked almost quickly. 'You think I'm trying to impress you or what?' Rex pretended to be so hurt that he looked away from her. He hoped to use the opportunity to find out if she cared about the way he felt.

'You're getting everything wrong, brother Rex,' she said quietly. 'If I had known you will feel so bad about this, I wouldn't have brought up the issue. I would simply stay away from here.'

'And you would enjoy seeing me hanging around with the ladies that are ready to take me to hell?'

'Brother Rex!' She laughed. He could not say if she was really amused. 'You've become a good Christian. I've told the pastor that.'

'If truly you know that,' he said indifferently, 'kudos to you. At least, you can see that your coming here had not been in vain. If you have to leave me at this point, you might have to account for my soul if I die in sins.'

'You talk as if you still commit sin. Do you still keep those ladies?'

'No but they are waiting for the lady that influenced and inspired me to throw me back into the mud.'

'Who wants to throw you back into the mud?'

'You!' he bellowed at her, pointing at her.

She roared with laughter at the way he said that.

He did not look amused at all as he allowed her to recover from the laughter. Then he said, 'the consciousness that you can come in here again anytime is enough to keep away me from being lured into sins.'

'That gives me the impression that you're more conscious of me than God. Am I right?'

'No.'

'Can you convince me you are not?'

'You can look at it this way. You represent godliness in my life, you realize that. If you're not there to put me through some things, by now I'll still be battling with drinks and women.'

'I get your point,' she said thoughtfully, thinking of what the pastor said some months ago. She could recall what he said vividly, "… He's your responsibility. For one, he's your student in the Sunday school and your child in the Lord. Secondly, I'm not the one that gives you the assignment. God did. He expects you to at least feed him until he's matured. You can tell God you cannot follow the soul he has placed in your care. You can give him your reason. He may understand your reason. I don't...."

Instead of her to get put off by what she once considered as undue generosity, she began to like him. Since he now understood what normally amused her, he made jokes that always sent her roaring with laughter. Before she knew it, she had become so conformable with him that she always looked forward to seeing him again.

If Rex was in love with Ann, he didn't seem to notice it nor think it was possible for him to win her heart. All he knew was that he attached great value to his friendship with her. He enjoyed every moment with her even if she didn't say a word throughout her visit. It gladdened him to see at her laughing at his jokes. He, however, began to sense that his life was taking a different trend. He got so occupied with the thought of Ann that he began to dream of her as his wife. The first dream he had was that they were together in the sitting room, playing love. The second time was the time two of them were together playing with two kids. He soon began to wish with his whole heart that these dreams came true. Of course, he dared not share dreams like that with anyone. During the general Sunday school, however, while taking a topic on how God directs his children, Rex asked, 'how does one know if God is directing someone?'

One of the Church elders who was taking the special general Sunday School said, 'one of the ways is found in the story of Abraham's servant who was sent to seek a wife for Isaac. He spoke to

God on how he wanted He to confirm of the lady He had chosen for Isaac. If you have been following the lesson very well, you'll understand that telling God how to specifically confirm what He wants you to do is one of the ways he can direct you. If you study the story of Gideon in Judges Chapter 6, you'll see that God confirms it to him that God was the one sending him to do the work which ordinary he would not have venture into if God had not directed him.

'Take a look at the story of Joseph. He had two dreams that pointed that he would be the head over his family. When his brothers sold him to the people going to Egypt, none of them know that they were actually following the plans God revealed to Joseph.'

There were more deliberations on the issue. Before the end of the lecture, the students were able to understand how God reveals his plans and how he directs his children to people through dreams and other ways. This of course, made Rex wondered if God wanted him to marry Ann. But then it was too fantastic for him to imagine Ann becoming his wife. Was God telling him through the dreams that he and Ann were going to set up a family together? Was Ann going to be his wife with all her intelligence, virtues, beauty, discipline, degree and other things that were so impressive about her? He wished with his whole heart that the dreams turned into realities.

He never stopped thinking of her all the time until he suddenly decided to risk telling her about the dreams. He would let her get the impression that he was just sharing what bordered him. He knew her to be a very humble lady. So telling her would neither make her intolerant of him and his dreams nor feel spiritually superior to think he was carnal.

About a month after the lesson on how God directs people, Ann called him on the phone to say, 'hi.'

'I'll like to see you, Sister Ann,' Rex told her immediately after the exchange of pleasantries. 'Would you rather want me to come over to your house or would you like to come here?'

'I'm sorry I can't spare the time right now. I'm really busy,' she said, 'I called just to inform you that we'll not see until the next two weeks.'

'Two weeks!' Rex screamed. 'I'll be sick before then.'

She laughed and said, 'you had better stop confessing negative things.'

'I'm serious, Sister Ann,' Rex said, 'I'm so eager to see you that I don't mind seeing you now.'

'What's so urgent in what you want to see me for?'

'It matters to me that I see you'.

Ann had always known Rex for making serious issues out of things that were of no relevance. Besides, he was good at finding reasons for meeting her though she was yet to know why. She asked, 'tell me what it is. I'll decide if it's so urgent.'

'I want to see you before I tell you,' he said.

'It doesn't look as if you really have anything to say. If you do you'll tell me now.'

There was a brief pause. Rex was reluctant to tell her but since she insisted to know, he said at last, 'it's about two strange dreams I had.'

'Well, what's the dream about?'

'I can't tell you now unless I see you,' he said.

'What's so important about the dreams?' Ann asked trying to get more information.

'I think it's about God's revelation we were taught in the Sunday school some weeks ago.'

'What does God reveal to you?'

'I can't tell you that on the phone.'

'I see,' Ann said slowly. She was very curious to know. Perhaps, she thought, it was about the issue she had been dodging for so long. 'Alright, I'll be there tomorrow in the evening when coming from the school.'

'Great!' he sounded very excited. 'I can't wait till then.'

'See you then,' she said and cut the line.

The following day, Rex came home on time to prepare for Ann's coming. His plan on how to tell her the dream seemed very promising. In fact, he had the feeling that he was going to have one of the most exciting moments of his life though he was not sure if he was taking the risk of ruining his friendship with Ann. Whatever the consequence of sharing his dream with her, he was prepared to take his chances with her.

He prepared some delightful meal for the two of them before she came. When she finally came, she appeared to be in a hurry leave.

'Please don't ruin my dinner. I've taken time to prepare this meal,' Rex said, 'so, please, do me the honour to dine with me.'

Reluctantly she went to the dinning table, sat down opposite him and prayed briefly and silently over the meal. She took some of the food before she went back to the sitting room.

When they sat down, she said, 'well?'

Rex looked thoughtful as he said, 'the two dreams I had is about you and me.'

Ann pretended to be very surprised.

'I don't want you to be offended by it, please,' Rex said quickly. 'And I don't want you to pick me up on that. The dreams are what I actually had. So if I'm wrong about my thoughts, I want you to simply correct me or tell me what to do.'

She shrugged. 'All right,' she said, softening her stare just to relieve him.

'I dreamt,' he continued, 'that the two of us were playing love in a sitting room.' He studied her face.

She did not register any surprise again.

'The second one is that the two of us were playing with our two children,' he said, breaking the uncomfortable silence.

She was expressionless.

Rex was anxious to know what was in her mind. He added, 'I had the dreams some weeks ago. I didn't tell you on time because I'm scared of the consequences of telling you?'

She snorted. 'What consequences were did you anticipate?'

'I don't know really....' Silence trailed his voice.

She said after a while, 'you don't want me to pick you up for these dreams. So I won't.'

'Thank you. I thought if I tell you, you will think I'm trying to make you my girlfriend since I don't have any good image before you.'

'You're wrong, you know,' she said. 'I never had any bad impression about you.'

'So what do you think about the dreams?'

'I think you should pray, brother Rex,' she said and stood up.

He looked at her for a long time. 'You mean you're not going say anything about this?'

'I just told you to pray.'

'That's all you're going to say?'

'Can you give a hint of what you expect me to say?' she asked indifferently.

'I expect you to tell me if it is possible or not.'

'It depends if the dreams are from God or not.'

'It's possible they're from God, isn't it?' he asked eagerly.

'Brother Rex,' she said impatiently, 'don't give me the impression that you cook up these dreams. So let's pray about it. Okay?'

He nodded, smiling at her. 'I did not cook up the dream.'

'I'll have to confirm that first. So you need to pray for it to be confirmed to me by God.'

'And if it is confirmed as the will of God...'

19

She was silent, looking beautiful as she thought of how to reply him. He thought she was a real beautiful queen. Tall, light complexioned and slim. Beauty was trademarked all over her.

He stood up, trying to play the man. 'Don't you care about me at all?'

'If I don't care about you,' she replied almost quickly, 'I wouldn't be here. You know that, don't you?'

'You care for me the way you care for your Sunday school students.'

'You're different, Brother Rex,"

'I'll like to know what makes me different,' he said, determined to push her hard.

'I like you,' she said laconically.

'See what I mean? If "like" is what you can use to distinguish the difference, how would you describe your feelings for other students?'

'You can borrow me the word if you don't mind.'

'You're a college professor. So you don't need anyone to borrow you words before you can describe your feelings.'

'This is not making sense,' she said. 'I'm not here to talk about feelings but your dreams.'

'Well, we have to talk about feelings now because you don't seem to care about the way I feel - I mean the feelings I have for you.'

'This is all about your feelings, right?'

He simply did not know where he got the courage to keep pushing his luck with her. 'It is also about yours. The point is the words "I like you" are not what I expect from someone I'm crazy about.'

She looked at his serious face for a long time before she burst out laughing.

That made him relaxed. 'If I'm really to describe my feelings for you, I'll say I love you.'

She knew she had to get out of the place if she did not want to betray her feelings by revealing it to him. She made towards the door. 'We'll talk about this later.

He went to block her way. 'Let's trash this out now once and for all.'

She smiled at him before she asked, 'which words would you rather want me to use now?' she asked. She was really impressed by his determination to know how she felt about him. She was also captivated by his gestures and looks.

'What's wrong in telling me you love me if you do?'

'Now you're getting impossible...' She stopped short when he frowned.

'Pretense and hypocrisy are members of the same family,' he said. 'If you pretend you don't care about someone, you appear either hypocritical or unloving. If you don't want me to have any of those impressions about you, I need to know if you love me.'

She looked thoughtful for a while before she said, 'even if I love you as you seem so sure, I can't do things outside the will of God. You know that, don't you?'

He looked confused for a while. He nodded and confessed, 'you got me there. I'll let you go off the hook today but when next I have the chance to talk about this with you, I'm not going to let you go that easy.'

She laughed. 'I wonder what makes you think you can get me.'

'The dreams,' he said quickly.

'Not every dream comes to pass, you know.'

'This will come to pass,' he replied. He seemed to have gotten the fact that the dreams were revelations from God. 'I've got God on my side and he will hand you over to me willy-nilly.'

'I'm out of here before you rape me.' She walked out of the house.

He roared with laughter. He continued to laugh as he followed her to where she packed her car.

THREE

Ann and Rex consciously or unconsciously entered into a marriage courtship. They became so fond of each other that they exchanged gifts nearly every week. Rex took every opportunity to spend a fortune on Ann. He even proposed to buy her a car. When she rejected the offer, he secretly began to build a house to give her a pleasant surprise. He was a senior officer in one of the richest oil companies in Nigeria. So money was not a problem to him. He had more than enough as benefit nearly every month. He was always paid in hard currency whenever he traveled overseas on courses.

Things, however, soon began to fall apart with Ann and Rex' relationship after he completed the house.

Unknown to Ann, Rex has not completely broken his relationship with Funmi. Just as Funmi had promised him the day he sent her out of the house when Ann came for a visit, she fought her way back into his life though it was not so easy. He seemed so involved with Ann that she could hardly get his attention again.

On the day one of Rex's friends was celebrating his birthday, however, Funmi staged a come back. She had gone to the birthday in a very beautiful and seducing dress, knowing very well that he would be there.

Rex was in the company of some of his friends who were taking some assorted drinks, including beer. Although he had told them that he was now born-again, they didn't really believe him.

'If you are now born again, why coming to party?' one of them challenged him. 'Or probably you're a social born-again Christian.' He poured some beer into a glass cup. 'How about taking this for a new life in Christ Jesus?'

The rest laughed.

Funmi who was familiar with his friends later went to join Rex and his friends at their table. Apart from Rex, everyone cheered the lady. The man sitting beside Rex quickly vacated his seat for her. As she sat beside him, everyone cheered again. 'You are going to be the wife of a pastor,' one of them said to her.

Although Rex thought of leaving the gathering but he could not

22

leave for the fear of being ridiculed by his friends. He pretended not to be offended and took the soft drink he had requested for.

A bottle of brandy was ordered for by the group. Funmi poured some inside a glass for herself and poured some into Rex's glass of soft drink before he could protest. Not wishing to make scene, he sipped some of it. All the while, he was thinking of how to get out of the place.

When it was getting a little dark, he stood up and said, 'well, guys, I have to go home now.'

'We are supposed to be here till dawn,' one of them said.

'I don't have the stamina,' he said. As he stood up, Funmi who was slightly drunk pulled him down. She pulled her arm around his neck, clutching him tightly. He knew what she was up to but he was determined to resist falling into her trap. She pressed herself harder against him as he attempted to push her away, trying to avoid creating a scene.

'If you are drunk, you better go home instead of trying to mess up yourself,' he growled at her.

'Hmm ... I want you, darling,' she whispered into his ear. 'Please, take me home.'

The temptation was getting too much for Rex to resist. He could not remember when last he got so close to a lady since his relationship with Ann began.

He tried hard to push her away but she cleaved to him like a child cleaving to her mother.

She soon began to arouse his urge to take her to bed. That day, they went home together to make love. Since she was able to seduce him that day, it was a lot easier to lure him to bed. She went to his flat once in a while for fun. All she had to do to seduce him was to hug him tightly before he resisted her.

Then one day, while it was raining heavily around six p.m. Ann was stranded on the way from the University. Her car suddenly got faulty on the way. Fortunately for her, the closest place she could get someone to help her was Rex's. She called his number but his line was not reachable. She decided to walk down to the place.

She managed to push the car to a save place, took her umbrella and locked the doors. She walked to Rex's flat. It was not really a long walk. So she got there within twenty minutes, feeling so chilly that she could not wait to get a shelter. By then, the lonely street was virtually deserted.

When she got to Rex's flat, she quickly reached out for the door bell and pressed it. When there was no response, she opened the door. It was not locked. She hoped he was at home. He was the only one that could take her to her house fast.

She entered the sitting room. There was no one around but she could hear the sound of a radio, coming from his bedroom. She dropped her bag on the sofa and went towards the bed room.

'Hello... Is anyone home?'

'Who is that? Rex asked form inside in a sleepy voice.

'Come out and see who,' she said.

The door was opened at last after a long delay. Rex stood by the door of his room. He wore shorts, looking slightly drunk. He gasped with surprise when he saw her.

Ann was so shocked to see him like that that she was speechless. This was not the Rex she knew. The one she knew had changed into a responsible and gentle man. The one she knew was a devoted Christian. 'What's happening?' she asked him in disbelief. But then a bigger surprise awaited her when she heard Funmi asking, 'who is that, Rex?'

Ann was stunned for along time, uncertain whether to go in and see the lady that was sharing the man she had hoped to so set up her family with or to turn back and leave immediately. Impulsively, she pushed Rex slowly out of the way and went in. It was the same lady she had met with him the first day she paid him a visit. She was lying under a bed sheet on the bed with bare chest which suggested she was naked underneath. For a moment, she was speechless, staring at the lady as if she was a strange creature. The situation didn't seem quite real to her. Rex, whom she had testified before everybody in the church that he was now a believer had gone back to his vomit.

'It's you again,' Funmi said, jumping on her feet. This was her chance - perhaps the only chance she had to take her man back from her. 'As you can see, I still have my guy though you tried to take him from me. You can go and look for yours elsewhere....'

'I'm sorry to intrude,' Ann said. 'I will never intrude again.

She closed the door and faced Rex. 'I thought you have changed. I could have vouched that you've changed....'

'I... I can explain this, Ann....'

She waved at him. 'There is no need. It looks to me now as if I've been wasting my time with you. You will never change. I am sorry to go this far into your personal life. I'll never do that again. The only thing I feel I owe you now is prayers. I cannot offer you anything more.'

Ann was so upset she could not think of anything but to get out of the house.

As she moved towards the door, Rex recovered from the surprise at seeing her. 'Y-you are going in the... the rain.'

'Never mind,' Ann said. She quickly got out of the house and slammed the door. She felt like bursting into tears. She forgot to take the handbag she left in the sitting room but she picked the umbrella she put outside and went into the street. She could no longer feel any cold as her emotion had taken over all her senses.

Meanwhile, Rex sat down on the edge of the couch, feeling perplexed. The worst that had ever happened to him since he became a Christian was for Ann to witness him messing around with another lady after having gone so far in their relationship and after having convinced her and himself that he was now born-again.

Rex went into the room. Funmi was still on the bed, feeling a little happy that the lady that was driving him frenzy had seen them together again. She knew by now, if the lady was as decent as she seemed, she was not expected to have anything to do with him again. If she would not have anything to do with him, she stood a chance to captivate him again. In fact, whenever she was ready for marriage, she would simply get pregnant and send her family to him to threaten him that if he didn't marry her, he would face serious spiritual attack. But then she was not yet ready for marriage.

Rex silently went to pick her clothes on the floor and threw them at her. She looked at him with surprised expression. 'I want you to please go home,' he said.

'What do you mean?' she snapped. 'It's raining outside.'

'A lady who means the whole world to me just walked into it. I don't see why you who mean nothing but a catastrophe to me should not go in there.'

'You really mean I mean nothing to you,' she asked, pretending to be hurt.

'You mean nothing but a catastrophe. Don't you hear that?' he asked. 'You are the devil in my life.'

'How have I become the devil?'

'I don't have time to argue with you. Just get lost.'

'I can't walk in the rain.'

'So what happens if you can't walk in the rain?' he asked curtly.

'I'm sleeping here.'

'That's a joke. I own this house. I decide who stays and who leaves.'

She glared at him. 'I'm going nowhere.'

'I can bet it with you that you will find yourself in the street by the time I'm through with you,' he growled at her. 'Do you want me to call the security man to throw you out or you'll like to go the easy way?'

She sprang up. 'What did the lady give you?' she asked. 'You met me first...'

'Shut up,' he said. 'I don't want to see you here again.'

'What do you mean?'

'What I said. I just discovered that you are a devil in the flesh of a lady that is out to kill, to steal and to destroy me.'

'You've been calling me the devil after you've used me the way you like,' she said, looking steadily at him. 'Well, the devil in the flesh of a lady is pregnant. She is carrying your child and she is setting up a family with you whether you like it or not.'

Rex hesitated for a while. Although he knew she was lying, he could not quite find what to tell her. He said, 'even if you are pregnant, you might have to prove who the real father is among your numerous boyfriends.'

That really burnt her. 'You are my only boyfriend!'

He laughed angrily. 'In that case, you really don't have any boyfriend and you might have to tell people that the child is a bastard.'

'The pregnancy is yours!' she stormed.

'You'll need to prove that with the DNA screening in the law court later,' he said. 'Meanwhile, I don't want to ever set my eyes on you. If you dare come to this place, you'll be sorry.' He pointed to the door. 'Get out.'

She put on her clothes and then turned to him. 'I need some money for my transport.'

He smiled to himself before he went to give her some money. It was a large sum of money. The amount would at least pay her off his life, which she had turned into a miserable one. She took the money and went away without saying anything. She knew wher she has been defeated.

Ann was walking back to her car, feeling so frustrated and angry that she was no longer conscious that her cloth was wet and her body was freezing in the rain. She could not imagine herself getting hooked up in a web of mess, planning to set up a family with a hypocrite who pretended to be a born-again Christian. This was a nightmare, she thought. 'God,' she cried within herself, 'how could you get me into this mess?'

She decided that moment that even if God actually meant them for each other, she would not have anything to do with him. 'Lord...,' she muttered to herself. She really needed to get home fast and weep. Yes, she would weep for herself and the hypocrite she had agreed to marry. Then she thought of how to get home. She would have to hire a taxi-cap since, as far as she was concerned, getting help from Rex was out of question. Getting a taxi that would take her home was what she ought to have done in the first place but the joy of seeing him was what made her went to him. Even then, she was almost sure the whole of her Israelite journey was designed by God so that she could catch him in the vomit.

It was when she got to where she parked her car that she realized she had left her bag in Rex' place. She was really mad at herself. She leaned against the car and began to cry. She would have to go back to the horrible place to get it! Already, she was sick and tired of the entire environment that was so full of cold and mess. She desperately needed a warm place to cry.

She left the car again and made her way to Rex's flat. Water was already dripping from her body when she got there.

Rex had locked the door the moment he sent Funmi out. Ann had to press the door bell twice before he heard it. He went to the door and asked, 'who is it?' he asked.

Ann felt so furious and frustrated that she didn't know when she screamed, 'open the goddamned door and give me my bag!'

Rex opened the door at once when he heard her voice. He knew he had to seize the opportunity to tell her he was sorry but how he would convince her that he was not a hypocrite was a big question.

She swept passed him to take the bag where she had left it and attempted to rush out. Apparently, she was not in the mood to listen to his excuses. Rex quickly went to block her way. 'Ann ....'

'Get out of my way!' she screamed.

'Ann, I am begging you in the name of Jesus,' he said. 'I ...I know I am a wretched sinner but ... you can help me if... if you want to.'

She looked steadily at him. 'Please, don't make me sin against God by condemning you. So I'm begging you too to let me go - now!'

To her surprise, she saw tears running down his eyes.

'You don't know how much I am hurt because I .... I betrayed you and God. God knows I want to please him but the devil lured me into it.'

Ann snorted. 'I wonder why people attribute their wrongs to the devil. The devil forced you to drink alcohol, the devil brought back that lady you told me you've cut off with. He took her to your bed - give me a break, Rex! I'm not your kind. We don't belong to each other.'

She paused, expecting him to react to the holier-than-thou

attitude which she deliberately exhibited. That seemed to be the best way to show him he was deep in the mud and she could not possibly reach out to him again.

There was silence. Instead of reacting to what she said, he looked more dejected and hopeless. His tears flowed more freely. She was really moved by what seemed like a sincere repentance. Even when she was so full of anger that she was ready to tell him to go right straight to hell, she still felt like giving him the second chance. But then, she thought, come what may, before she gave him the second chance, he would have to prove that he had not only changed but also would not get involved with any lady again. How he would do that was his problem, not hers.

'How can I possibly help you when you have strange women in your life?'

'She's the only one troubling my life and I've asked her to go... and never to come back.'

'That's what you said the first time I met her with you,' she said.

'This time I've decided not to have anything to do with her.'

'I'm sorry, Rex.'

'Y-you mean you'll not help me?'

She shook her head slowly. 'Only God can help you. I've played all the roles God wants me to play in your life. So the only sensible thing to do right now is to leave you alone.'

'And then allow me to go to hell?' he interrupted.

Again there was silence.

'That's your choice,' she replied after a while.

He frowned. 'My choice? How can I choose hell?'

'You'll tell me the answer because I don't know why you choose a life that can take you there.'

He said in a whisper, 'I thought you care about me.'

'Yeah, I do,' she replied. 'But when you take the love of God and my love for your soul for granted, you risk too many things, including your eternity.'

He looked thoughtful. 'So I'm beyond the reach of God.'

'I didn't say that,' she said quickly. 'What I'm saying is found in Isaiah chapter 59 verses 1 and 2. That passage was once your memory verse, remember. It says, "Behold, the LORD'S hand is not shortened, that it cannot save; neither his ear heavy, that it cannot hear: But your iniquities have separated between you and your God, and your sins have hid his face from you, that he will not hear." It doesn't occur to you that God sees you and he'll expose you one day

28

when you were bringing the lady into your house?'

Rex was so hurt that he leaned against the door. He asked after a while, 'what do you want me to do now?'

'Ask God to forgive you. I know he will because he is a merciful God.'

'What would you do to me?'

'I'll pray for you.'

'Do you want me to help you dry your clothes before I take you home?' he asked.

She could see that he was getting irrational. She wondered what made him think she would accept any of his offers. 'No thanks. I can manage.'

'How about taking you home?'

'I don't need anything from you,' she said. 'I'll like to be on my way now if you would let me go.'

'You have not forgiven me, have you?' he asked.

'If I've not, I wont exchange any word with you but the truth is you have to prove it to me that you're the responsible man I thought. That is going to be very hard to do because I no longer have enough confidence in you that can make me build the kind of relationship you want me to build. So you have to pray to God to give me that kind of confidence.' She smiled at him for the first time. 'At least, we don't have to pretend as if we are in courtship now because we are not.'

'Oh, my God,' he said in whisper. 'I can't survive this.'

'You'll survive. Good day, brother Rex. We'll see some other time.' She quickly got out of the house before he had time to reply.

He slowly closed the door and went to sit down sorrowfully to ponder over his life.

He knew that his relationship with Ann was still in a mess if not completely ruined. He wanted to talk to Jesus about it. He wanted to tell him he was sorry. He wanted to promise him he would not do it again. But then, how could he talk to Jesus when he was so filled with filthiness - with a mouth stinking of liquor.

Not knowing what to do, he locked the door back and went to bed in sorrow.

FOUR

Ann sat under the tree in front of her flat in a lonely area one bright Saturday. She had been feeling sorrowful since the day she discovered Rex was still involved with the lady. She didn't quite get the picture of what was happening in her life. God told her through the mouth of ministers that the man he had prepared for her was in Nigeria. She came to the country and met Rex who, from many indications, provec to be the man for her. Instead of growing into a strong Christian that would set up an adorable family and powerful ministries with her, he was still battling with sins. If not for his apparent repentance, she would have called it a quit with him and look else where for a husband.

She had no idea how long she had sat under the tree before someone drove a car and parked in front of her flat. She stood up and hurried to the visitor. The visitor was her cousin who lived in Britain.

'Ann!' John, her cousin said when he saw her. He was a tall and handsome man with far complexion and sharp intelligent eyes.

'Hay, John!' she cried excitingly. He grabbed and kissed her in the cheek. 'What a surprised visit!' she said as she led him to the house.

'Uncle told me you're now in Nigeria. So I told him he should give me your address. I promised to see you when I come to see my mother in Lagos.' He followed her into the finely furnished sitting.

'I kept wondering why I never heard from you for ages,' she said. 'You never sent me mails as before.'

'Yeah,' he said, 'I'm sorry about that,' he said. 'I was kind of busy through out last year. Unlike in the States, Europe is rather full of struggle.'

'What can I offer you?'

'Soft drinks would do.' he said.

'I'll get it for you,' she said and stood up to go and get it in the refrigerator in the kitchen.

'I brought you a present,' John said, also going to get it for her in his car.

'Oh, really?'

When he came back, she was waiting for him with the drinks in the

30

sitting room. He handed the package to her. It was a new lap top. 'I felt you'll appreciate it since you're not likely to get that type in Nigeria so easily.'

Ann anxiously opened and examined the package. She felt so happy that she went to hug him. 'Thank you so very much! God must have told you to bring this to me!' Just then, Rex came in through the door which John left open when he brought the present.

Rex gestured aimlessly. 'I'm ... sorry to interrupt. I found the door ... open.'

'It's ok, gentleman,' John said. He looked at Ann, expecting her to formally introduce them. When she didn't, he stretched out his hand to him in handshake. 'I'm John.'

Rex forced himself to smile and shook his hand. 'I'm Rex.' He looked at Ann who looked rather indifferent. She could read it at once through his gestures that he was suspicious of her relationship with John and that really served him right.

She gestured him to a seat. 'You can have your seat.'

'Oh, no,' Rex said quickly. 'We'll see later.'

'Am I...' John attempted.

Ann interrupted, thinking he was about to erase the suspicion that they were in love. 'Oh, no, honey. Let him go. I don't have much time for him today anyway.'

Rex could not hide his annoyance. He forced a smile again before he waved at John. 'See you again, John.'

'I hope it'll be soon,' John said as a matter of courtesy. He knew they were not likely going to see since he planned to leave the country the following day.

'I hope so,' Rex said and left the house immediately.

'Who is the guy?' John asked.

'He's one of our Church members.'

'He seems to be in love with you.'

Ann smiled. 'You are right.'

'I hope he knows I'm your cousin.'

'No. Why?'

'Ann. The guy may be jealous. He saw you hugging me. The meaning of hugging here means something entirely different.'

'Let him feel jealous. I don't care.'

'I care,' he said and added jocularly. 'I don't want a guy running after me with a double barrel gun!'

Ann roared with laughter.

They chatted for about an hour before he left. He promised to see her again as soon as possible.

When Rex got home that day, his head was so full. Ann whom he respected so much was not only involved with another man but playing love!

He could not believe his eyes when he saw her hugging him. Was that the way Christians were supposed to behave? Were they supposed to be hypocritical about their faith in Christ, doing something contrary to what they professed? If Ann whom he loved, respected and adored so much could be keeping a man, he could as well go back to his perverted ways of life and then became hypocritical about his faith too.

He went to the telephone at once to send a message to Funmi that he would like to see her. As he picked the telephone, something held his hand. 'Why not go to Ann? You love her, don't you? Funmi will only ruin your life the more.'

He dropped the telephone at once and went to take his car key. He drove to Ann's flat.

Ann was reading in the sitting room, preparing for the Sunday school when the bell rang.

'The door is open,' she said.

Rex came in, looking angrily at her.

'Hello, Rex,' Ann said without moving from where she was writing.

'Ann,' he said without hesitation. 'Why are you so hypocritical about your faith in Christ?'

'What do you mean?' she asked. She did not even bother to look at him. She knew exactly what he was talking about.

'You know deep inside you that you are not a Christian.'

'You really think so?' she asked.

He was annoyed at her indifferent attitude the more. 'Of course, you know you're a hypocrite.'

'Why not leave the judgment to God,' she shot at him, 'and mind your business?'

'You mean it's not my business to… to question the closeness between you and John or whatever he calls himself?' he asked, looking both jealous and angry.

Ann looked at him, determined to press him to the wall. He must prove to her that he really felt the same thing she felt when she saw him with the lady.

'What's your business in my affairs?' she asked.

'So you haven't forgotten what happened the other day, have you?' he asked after a brief silence. 'We are supposed to be planning for our marriage.'

There was silence. She knew he did not take her seriously when she told him their relationship was over. 'You seem to have forgotten what I told you that day,' she said. 'I'll spell it out to you. If there was really any relationship between us, there's none now. I wasn't really planning any marriage with you,' she said. 'I was watching you. I can't put up with a man like you.'

He was tempted to tell her that she was not in the position to point out the black spot in him since there was a black spot in her too but he did not fall into the temptation. Instead, he went to sit down slowly and dejectedly on the couch. 'Oh, Ann, why are you doing this to me? Why don't you help me instead of putting me more into bondage of sin?'

He stood up and went to sit on the table facing her. 'Your reaction to the whole issue almost cause me to invite the lady to my flat again.'

Ann looked steadily at him. They looked at each other's face. Both of them could see love and charm in each other's face.

'Ann,' he said in a stiff voice. 'I know I have sinned against God and I've asked for forgiveness of my sins as you advised me. For you to get involved with another man without seeing anything wrong in doing that is a surprise to me and a stumbling block in my Christian life.'

As he was talking the door bell rang. She went to open the door. It was John again but he was out of Rex's view.

'I forgot to give you the letter Dora's ask me to deliver to you.'

'Oh, thanks,' she said, taking the letter from him. He was about to go away when she said; 'wait a minute, John. I'll like to introduce you to Rex by myself.'

John entered the sitting room and saw Rex, looking expressionlessly at them.

John looked at her and said, 'be nice and make the proper introduction, please.'

She laughed. 'Come here, Rex,' she said, beckoning at him.

Rex silently went to join them by the door.

Ann smiled at him. There was no use hurting him again. After all, it was apparent that both of them loved each other. 'John, guess what? Rex happened to be my jealous fiancé. You were right to say he was mad to see me hugging you. He doesn't know you are my cousin.'

John laughed so heartedly that he went to throw himself on one of the seat. 'I knew it.' He looked at her. 'I knew you were working him up when you didn't introduce us to each other. I wonder why you are doing that.' He looked Rex. 'She plays naughty girl at times but she is a very good a material for your family set up. You're lucky to have her, believe me.'

Rex smiled at him. 'I believe you, brother,' he said, looking at Ann. He was obviously pleased to hear that.

John continued, 'she my uncle's daughter. So don't fal for her trick again. I really don't know what she planned to achieve by making you feel jealous.'

'I promise you I won't let her wont fool me again,' Rex replied, still smiling at him.

'I hope we are friends.'

'Yeah...'

'So what do you do?'

'I'm a chemical engineer.'

'You have a company of your own or you work with somecne.'

'I work with Mobil Oil Company.'

'That's good place to work,' John said excitedly. 'I'm sure you'll look after my cousin.' He looked at her. 'She's an adorable little creature. Don't you think?'

'John, how dare you call me a creature!' Ann said.

He looked at Rex again. 'Like I said, you'll find out that you're a lucky guy to have her. I'm sure you love her, don't you?'

'Yeah,' Rex said.

'That explain why you were jealous. Boy, I like jealous guys! It's rare these days to see a man feeling jealous unless he loves the lady,' he said, getting up to move towards the door again. 'I wish I have time to chat with you guys. I've wasted time already. See you again.' He waved to them and left almost immediately.

Rex was happy to know that he was wrong all the while to think that Ann and John where lovers.

There was along silence after John had gone.

'Why did you give me the impression that the man was your boyfriend?' he asked.

'Well,' she said, 'there was no other way to make you realize how wrong it is for you to get involved with another lady.'

'You know,' he said in a whisper, 'you made me feel ashamed of myself.'

'It's okay now,' she said. 'You're still who you are to me.'

'And who am I to you?' he said.

'Are you teasing me or what?'

'Oh, no, Ann,' he said. 'I used to feel joyous when you let me know that you're conscious that we are in a marriage courtship.'

'Well, you heard how I introduced you to John.'

He smiled, looking more handsome. 'Yeah,' he said. 'I am happy to know that at least you say I'm your fiancé.' He paused to look at her beautiful face. 'I have a surprise for you, love.'

'What's the surprise?'

'The surprise is at Victoria Island,' he said. 'Would you like to come and see it?'

Within some minutes they were on their way to the house Rex had built without her knowledge. It was a splendid house - so exquisite that Ann was dazed when he declared that the house belonged to them.

'That's where we'll set up our family,' he said.

Tears of joy filled her eyes. All the while she had been thinking that God didn't quite show interest in her, he had been working for her good.

'Guess what!' Rex said, using her slang. 'I want us to get married next year. Do you like that?'

Ann smiled. 'I think I like it.'

'If you do, say the miracle words,' he said cheerfully.

'I love you,' she said quietly, smiling at his face that was shining with joy and excitement.

THE UNROMANTIC LOVE BIRDS

ONE

They met in the school located in one of the then Western Region of Nigeria. At that time, students learned to live the life of elites. No doubt Charles and Funke fell in love the moment they set eyes on each other.

She was eating snacks during the leisure hour under a tree, looking or seeming to be engrossed in the volleyball game between the medical and the engineering students.

Funke, a tall, light, beautiful and graceful lady had seen Charles among the volleyball players. He was reasonably handsome and seemingly charismatic. He has the features of an athlete. Indeed he was an athlete. He was volleyball star in the university. Something unusual had attracted her attention to him even though she had met him a couple of times. As an English student, she loved his command of English language. She expected him to be good at English anyway, having heard that he was one of the most brilliant students that graduated from King's College, one of the most the prestigious secondary schools in the whole Africa.

The volleyball game ended. Charles looked round for his friends and caught Funke's sight at a distance. He quickly made up his mind to go and accompany her, having been trying to be alone with her for long.

'Hi,' he said cheerfully as he approached her, smiling.

'Hi,' she replied indifferently.

Without requesting for permission, he sat beside her on the wooden bench and sighed. 'You enjoy the game?'

'Hmmm,' she replied, 'your performance was not too bad. I suppose those medicos are only good in the theatre.'

He chuckled. 'You should have told them that. What about the engineering students?'

'You're not too good either,' she replied. 'The only advantage you had over them was the two strikers on your side. Your defense was not as poor as theirs.'

'You're a critic, Funke,' Charles said. 'And there's one thing more to that.'

'What?' she asked wearily.

He deliberately hesitated for a long time.

'What is it?' she asked again, looking at him.

'Can I whisper it into your ear?' Charles asked.

'Why should you do that?' she asked. 'No one is listening.'

'If you don't give me your ear, I won't say it.'

Smilingly, she turned her ear to his face. He loved the scent coming from her body. He whispered into the ears, 'you're beautiful, Funke. I'm crazy about you.'

She burst out laughing and said, 'you're mad! Better tell those medicos to take you to the theatre to examine your head.'

He laughed with her. 'What's wrong in being in love?'

'Charles,' she said, 'you know you cannot be in love with me. Even if you don't have a girlfriend, I have a boyfriend.'

'You lied!' Charles said quickly. 'I've already inquired about you before I fell into the deep river of love with you.'

'I hope you will not get drown,' she laughed.

'It doesn't matter if I do as long as it is because of you.' He laughed with her.

Funke who knew that Charles was aware of her love for him did not play the game of "hard-to-catch" with him for too long before she agreed to become his girlfriend.

******

Charles was twenty-three years old when he began to court with Funke who was then twenty. Both of them had a very high moral background. So they never made love to each other throughout the time they were in school as practiced by most lovers in the campus. Even when they eventually attempted it shortly after their graduation, Charles discovered that Funke had never met with any man before. Of course, that commanded his respect for her the more. They soon began to plan for their marriage.

It wouldn't take Charles a long time to discover that Funke was from a very wealthy family. Her mother was kind, loving and very generous. She was also very disciplined and stern. She ensured that all her children who were mainly females were also disciplined. Her attitude towards any man falling in love with any of her children was stormy if not aggressive. So when she heard that Charles was in love with Funke, she became impatient to meet and warn him never to have anything to do with her daughter.

One day, she went to Charles' friend called Femi to inquire about him. Coincidentally, Charles was with Femi at the time she came to lodge her complaint. Although she knew Charles by name, she had no idea how he looked like.

'Do you know the man called Charles?' Funke's mother asked Femi.

Femi looked at Charles and asked, 'do you know the person?'

Charles nodded. 'Yes, I know him. He's an engineer and a friend of mine who works as a civil servant.

'My dear,' she said, 'when you see him, please warn him I don't want him to mess around with my daughter again. I can only release my daughter to the man who really wants to marry her.'

'I will deliver your message, Ma,' Charles said. As soon as Funke's mother left the room, the two men burst into laughter

'Men,' Femi said. 'Mama is telling a cat to keep watch over her meat.'

With that, it became apparent that they have to be meeting without anyone who may inform Mama about it.

The following week, Charles and Funke met at Femi's house which became the place of their secret meeting. They had a long chat before Charles said, 'I would like to make pledges to you, Funke. I will love and honor you with all my heart. I will protect your interest at all cost even at the expense of my personal convenience till death parts us. I will also vest my total love on you and would not entertain or accommodate the love of another lady in my heart. And I will honor and respect every member of your family, irrespective of age, position and character.'

These pledges were actually borne out of Charles experience as member of a polygamous family. In the earlier days of Charles' life, he learned a lot of bitter lessons from his father. As it was common practice in the ancient days in Africa, most men, especially those who were blessed with a lot of farmlands have as many wives as their financial resources could accommodate. Even then, it was commonly believed that the more wives a man has, the more family members he would have to work on the farm; causing him to be richer. When a man became old, he could take a young woman for a wife and this invariably, as it was believed, would prolong his life. If the senior wife became old, she automatically got a retirement while the younger wife took her place as the bed mate.

When Charles was thirteen years old, his mother who was the senior wife had a hideous conflict with one of the younger wives called Mama Kola. She was a beautiful woman with romantic features that captivated the entire heart of Charles' father. She was his favourite wife and he could do anything to protect her interest. Mama Kola was very conscious of the special position she occupied in the heart of Charles' father. She therefore used it as machinery to rule the entire household. It was established by customs and order at that time that the senior wife was next to the husband in ruling the household but Mama Kola defied the norms by her disregard for everybody including Charles' mother.

On the day the hideous conflict occurred, Charles' father was on the farm while his mother and Mama Kola were left at home with some other people. There was sudden exchange of heated words between the two women. When Charles' father returned home, Mama Kola was quick to narrate what had happened in his absence, hiding some truths that would implicate her and adding some lies that would make him get angry at Charles' mother.

Charles' father never border to find out the whole truth before he reacted. He called Charles' mother bounced on her, beating her mercilessly. The only people around then were Charles and his pregnant sister-in-law. Of course, none of them could rescue his mother from his father. So Charles who was too young and confused to help his mother watched the incident that would later influence his entire life. His sister-in-law was the only one that could render little help. She ran out of the compound, shouting for help. She succeeded in getting the neighbours into the house but before they could render any help, Charles' mother has sustained several injuries including dislocation of her vertebral column.

The incident was registered permanently in Charles' mind even up to the time he was making pledges to Funke.

In response to Charles' pledges, Funke who had no such experience that can influence her life said, 'I will love and give full respect to you as my husband and I will try to meet your needs and demands as much as possible. Secondly, I will be faithful. I will reserve myself totally for you and nothing will ever make me show interest in another man until death parts us.

Then the two decided to inform their families of their intention to get married.

TWO

The marriage ceremony was fantastic. Eminent personalities attended the wedding. It was really a memorable day for Charles and Funke. The most memorable moment of the wedding was the sermon given by one of the pastors that officiated on that day. He talked extensively on their marriage as if he knew what would come out of it.

'Marriage,' he said, 'is not the ceremony or the celebration that the couple had come together. It is the institution which the couple in question has formed together. In other words, it is living together in peace and harmony. The bedrock of every successful marriage is love, trust and mutual understanding. Any marriage that lacks any of these ingredients will definitely fail. We have seen marriages that were fabulously celebrated crumbling like a house of cards. Personally, I know of a marriage where the husband left the wife to be joined to another woman in another country just because he could not tolerate the wife.

'For a marriage to be truly successful, the following vital principles must be applied: Firstly, the husband must love his wife as Christ loved the church and gave His life for it.

'Secondly, under no circumstances must the husband be bitter against his wife. I used to wonder at some husbands who are bitter against their wives. Jesus gave us the commandment that the wife and the husband must be of one flesh. If couple has truly become one flesh, which person will say that he will cut off his head just because he has headache?'

There was soft laughter among the people.

'When you're bitter against your spouse, you're bitter against your very self. If the idea of divorce comes into your head, it means you want to divide your flesh into two. Who can survive that? You may survive it physically but you cannot survive it spiritually.

'The next principle is that the wife must submit herself unto her husband. Many women are unruly and heady. They hate to receive instructions from their husbands. It may be because they feel superior to them in one way or the other. It may also be because of their backgrounds. Some look down on the husbands as if they are not

41

capable of commanding them. You can check the house of such people. It is always on fire. Of course, this always affects the family.

'There was a man in my church. He was always active in the church and in the office before he got married. Few weeks after his marriage, he suddenly became reserved and somewhat unhappy. I intruded into this man's marital life because I love him to the extent that I cannot ignore him in that state. I later discovered that he had married a Jezebel. The woman showed him the other side of love. It was terrible. We prayed that God should restore the peace and joy of that man. Guess what happened. The wife died of fever when she traveled to her hometown. We didn't pray for her to die but when God saw that as the only way to answer our prayer, He took her away. The man had his peace back at last. When we asked him two years later when he would marry again, he said, "Pastor, let me recover from the first marriage."

The people again chuckled.

'You see, marriage could be a blessing and a curse, depending on the principles you use to pick and live with your wife. If you apply the scriptural principle, it will be well with your family.

'The next principle on how to have a successful marriage is tolerance. Husband and wife must selflessly tolerate each other. Many spouses are self-centered. They do not put their husbands or wives into consideration. Like I use to tell people, the worst character in a man is selfishness. It is selfishness that makes wives or husbands to lavish money on themselves at the expense of their families. You see, the women are good at playing that trick. When their husbands refuse to buy them what they want, they wait until it is bedtime. When the husbands want to make love to them, they would say, "well, darling, we'll make love on the condition that you buy me this or that." The husband may not have the money the wife wanted but he had to make a promise because he has to, you know, cool the tension of his body. If the man does not fulfill his promise, she begins to cause trouble in the house.

'Some husbands used to deny their wives of certain needs. Tolerance is the ability of both husband and wife to understand the need of each other and accommodate or meet it. I've seen so many marriages crumbling because of inadequate communications between the couples. Apart from that, they must tolerate the character of each other. Tolerance is very important in every relationship or marriage. A person who knows what can upset his or her spouse and yet goes ahead to do that thing is looking for trouble.

'The next point is the area of lovemaking. If you try to find out the causes of many divorces, you'll discover that they are attributed to this area of marriage. Any wife or even husband who believes that he or she can only offer herself or himself to the spouse only when he or she is in the mood to enjoy it is not a loving spouse. Love making ease the emotional tension of a person in most cases. If you starve your spouse of it, you are giving him or her good reason to go out and get it. I can assure you, he or she will get it outside and that will mark the beginning of the problem in that family.

'I remember a man who was dismissed in an office for an offence he had not committed. Guess what he did. He took his letter and went to his wife to make love. His wife did not co-operate with him. He burst out crying like a baby. She became agitated and asked what went wrong. He explained to her that he had been fired in the office and he hoped to get consolation from her. Quickly, she allowed him to make love to her. Can you believe that that was all that brought back the man's senses? He was able to handle the situation - perfectly well just because he got the consolation he wanted from his wife. Supposing his wife, out of frustration, had refused to let him touch her; he may go out to get what he needed at that time and may even get himself drunk. I don't need to tell you the implication of that

'The next area is sharing and bearing each other's burdens. You know that whatever happens to any part of the body affects all the parts. This is also applicable to married couples. Husband cannot isolate himself from his wife. If the wife is bordered by what is happening to her parents, the husband must be bordered too. The problem of a man is also his wife's and vice versa. All what I'm sharing with are scriptural principles. You can find the area of bearing one another's burden in the Book of Galatians chapter six verse two.

'Let's consider the area of disagreement. There is no such thing as relationship without conflict. At times, disagreement will arise. It's natural for conflict to occur. As the proverb says, 'tongue and teeth who respect each other do fight. You know what I mean? When the teeth are grinding the food like this "Munch, Munch," the tongue dare not play around at that time. When the tongue is rolling the food for the teeth to work on, the teeth dare not grind the tongue with it. But guess what happen when the teeth mistakenly crush the tongue, the whole body including the teeth reacts to it. Every part of the body feels the pain. The teeth will stop working immediately and begin to plead, "oh, I'm so sorry!" That's the relationship between the parts of the body. Once there is disagreement, the couple must find a way to resolve it. If

43

you are at fault, be humble enough to accept it and apologize. It is a sign of pride if a spouse refuses to accept his or her fault. It is a sign of humility if a spouse admit the fault that is not even his or hers. That type of humility is an impressive strength, which the devil cannot crush. It is better to wave your right as a wife or husband for the sake of peace than to claim it. You may claim your right and claim trouble with it. So couple must learn to be in constant agreement by finding ways to understand each other. Do not find any reason to disagree with him. If there is anything you want your spouse to do or understand, find the appropriate time to tell him or her with love. You can easily command the attention of a giant with love than to threaten him with a gun. You see, you'll not be able to command the giant again the moment you drop the gun. Also the couple must form the habit of praying together. This is a very formidable insulation against satanic influerce. It's a pity; the family altar in many marriages had been pulled down. Unknown to them, they have given invitation card to the devil to mess up their marriages. There should be family alter in every home where couples and their children can meet to pray and share the word of God together on a daily basis.

'Lastly, husband and wife must be faithful to each other in everything they do. They must have confidence in each other and allow God to be their consultant. They must not go to their families or friends who do not have any proof of godliness for advice. I've seen thousands and one cases of marriages that collapsed as a result of taking advice from such people. You see, when couples do things in common and they are faithful to each other, it will be impossible for anybody to come around and pull down the marriage with gossips.

'There was a man who gave a lady a ride in Lagos. The lady seemed to be stranded but, unknown to the man, she was a real troublemaker. So when it was time to get down from his car, she said she would not get down until he gave her certain amount of money. The man asked her why he has to give her money. She said, "what do you mean? For the past three days you have been taking me to hotels, sleeping with me without giving me a kobo. Now you're telling me to get out of your car." Guess what the man did. He took the lady home on the pretense that he was going to get her some money. When they got there, he handed her over to his wife. The lady repeated her story and the man's wife pull her neck and said she would kill her for lying against her husband. That was what saved the man from trouble.

'I told you earlier on that the bedrock of every successful marriage is love and trust. What brings trust is faithfulness. If the man is not faithful, he would have been in a big trouble. In fact, he would not have the courage to hand over the trouble maker to his wife.

When there's trust and faithfulness in the family, nobody can come around to scatter the family. I repeat: nobody....'

The Pastor soon completed the sermon, having established solid points in the minds of the couple and the people that were present at the marriage ceremony.

THREE

At the early stage of their marriage, Charles and Funke traveled to America in pursuit of their academic careers. They had their first and second children within the few years of their stay in the country. Both of them were boys. They soon returned to Nigeria and became highly placed citizens. Funke became a lecturer at a university while Charles set up a civil engineering company with three branches in three major cities of Nigeria.

They lived in Lagos where the family was blessed financially. There was peace throughout this period. After having one more child who was a female, Funke completely became unromantic. She no longer entertained any form of romance with Charles. She didn't see any need for it since they have had enough children. It seemed that she had been cooperating with Charles all the while because of the children she had hoped to get. Now that she had got the children she needed and she was almost forty, she saw romance as a messy game reserved for the youths. Besides, to Charles' detriment, she naturally hated romance. At this stage of their marriage, the journey began to get rough. Apart from series of trial and temptations, which Charles always faced, he soon discovered his incompatibilities with Funke in the area of romance. But he persevered, knowing fully well that he could not withdraw the pledges he had made to her before they got married. Occasionally, when Charles attempted to make love to Funke, she would say she was not in the mood. So he would have to wait endlessly for the time she would be in the mood. The poor sexual relationship between the couple threatened the stability of the marriage. He became so frustrated that he was forced to go and seek for advice from one of her friends called Ada. Funke and Ada had been friends since they were in secondary school.

'Well,' Charles said, 'actually, what I'm about to tell you is an embarrassment to me. But I feel I should tell you because it is something that can break my marriage with Funke. You see, I love my family and I don't desire anything like divorce.'

Ada who was very intelligent and sensitive was able to guess right

46

what was happening in the family even before he told her.

'Funke had been denying me some vital elements of marriage. For sometime now since she gave birth to Jude, she had ceased to be romantic. I cannot even touch her. Is that how married couple should live?'

Ada apologize Charles for Funke's shortcomings and promised to counsel her.

She later sent for Funke and began to appeal to her. 'Funke, you must not treat your husband this way. Very few people have the privilege to have the sort of man you have. If you have my type of husband, your marriage would have gone into history by now but thank God you don't. If I had not submitted to my husband, I would have been thrown out even without notice. If I'm out, another woman will become the step-mother of my children. Do you want that to happen to you? To be candid, a woman is created as help mate of the man and not man for woman. Whatever it will cost you to save your marriage, you better sacrifice it.

Funke promised to take to Ada's advice but she found it difficult to fulfill her promise. She has got so used to unromantic life that she was unwilling to change.

Charles went to seek for another advice from his close friend called Tony.

'I did all I could to help the situation,' Charles told Tony, 'but nothing worked.' He suggested that Tony should have a talk with Funke about it even though he knew she would not take to the advice, no matter how precious it was.

Tony was sympathetic but he blamed Charles for his predicament. 'My friend, no woman can treat me like that and still remain under my roof.'

'How can you say a thing like that, Tony?' Charles said. 'You know I love her and my children. How can I send her away and bring another woman into the house?'

'I'm not saying you should do what I said I would have done,' Tony said in defense, 'because you're not me; are you? Since you're not me, I suggest you should have a girlfriend secretly and save yourself from unnecessary burden of a heartless woman you call your wife. After all there are many fishes in the sea and very few fishermen to catch them.'

Charles thanked him for his candid advice but he was reluctant, if not scared to take to his advice. Having a girlfriend could cost him many things. Firstly, it would cause him to break his promises. It could

47

cost him the respect people accorded to him and lastly it could lead him to the practice polygamy, which he had been running away from. On the other hand, if he got himself a bed mate to complement Funke's intolerable sexual inadequacy, he would save himself the embarrassments of going about telling people what was going on in his family. Already, he was beginning to loose the dignity and the right to keep what was happening in his family a secret. The reasons for not taking to Tony's advice were very powerful but they were not strong enough to override the agony he was going through secretly. As a matter of fact and principle, if not for the love he has for his wife and children, he wouldn't have gone this far before he got as many girlfriends as he desired. He was in deep river of love which, sadly enough was not appreciated by his wife. Instead she made the river of love felt like river of mess and sorrow.

******

Funke's mother whom Charles fondly addressed as Mama has a big building in Lagos metropolis. There were many tenants living in the house with Mama. Among the tenants was a pretty lady called Rita. She was Mama's favorite tenant. She was submissive and loving. Mama treated her as though she was her daughter. Because Mama was naturally disc plined, she sternly guided her against men who might be interested in her just as she did to her biological children.

Charles' office was very close to where Rita worked. As the transportation in such a cosmopolitan city was always very hectic and sometimes frustrating, Rita intimated Mama to tell Charles to always give her a ride to the office in his car. Mama did as she requested. And so Rita has the privilege of not only riding in Charles' car but also to get close to him. Rumor soon began to spread that Charles was having a girlfriend. Charles was not bordered by the rumor since he had no mind of getting involved with any lady. Rita who probably must have sensed his secret agony, however, had a hidden agenda. She developed the habit of playing some tricks on Charles in other to win his heart. The rumor going around them helped her to set her machinery in order.

One day, she asked him to take her to a cinema house where a romantic film would be shown.

'Why asking me to take you there?' Charles asked.

'I wouldn't like to go to a public theatre alone,' she answered. 'You know as a young lady, I need to avoid falling into men's mischief. With you around, I'll be secured.'

'Why not ask your boyfriend to take you there?'

'I don't have a boyfriend she said shyly.'

Charles sensed that she was playing a game but he could not see how she would possibly win his heart if he didn't co-operate with her. He was determined not to play along with her though he felt obliged to go to the cinema house with her.

'Okay,' he said reluctantly, 'let's go.'

The cinema house turned out to be a very classic one. Only high quality films were exhibited at the place.

Rita led Charles who had not been to the place to a table at a corner. Soon the light was switched off and the film began.

Sitting beside each other as the romantic film progressed, their bodies began to ache for lovemaking. It was rather a big temptation for Charles who was sex starved to overcome. Most of the scenes in the film only reminded him of what he was missing in his married life.

Rita began to expect Charles' touch any moment as the film got to the climax. She even encouraged him to touch her by deliberately touching him with her bosom. At first, Charles did not react. He had to employ every effort he had to resist the temptation. She stole a glance at him. He caught her. Then, involuntarily, his hand went to her bosom and both of them began to explode with passion. They caressed each other until they could not wait for the film to end. There were rooms in the cinema house to be rented by people in Charles' and Rita's condition. Rita suggested that they should rent one of the rooms before they went back home. They rented the place for an hour and made love there. Charles who seemed not to have gotten so close to a woman for ages felt relieved of his sexual urge.

When they were leaving the cinema house, Charles felt so ashamed and guilty that he could not say anything or even look at Rita's face.

'It's a wonderful experience,' she said, trying to ease him of his guilt and embarrassment. It was indeed a very wonderful experience, considering the fact that he could not recall the last time he made love. But he knew he had to stop the relationship that was about to develop between him and Rita, at least, for Mama's sake. The elderly mother-in-law trusted him with everything. Having a relationship with the tenant she considered her own daughter was not only an insult to her pride but a downright betrayal.

49

He looked at Rita who looked bright probably because she had successfully gotten him to make love to her. He said, 'Rita, we must put an end to this.'

'What? I mean why?' She looked a little disappointed.

'You know I'm a married man,' he said sadly as if he regretted getting married. 'And my wife's mother happens to see you as her daughter. It's a betrayal to be doing a thing like this.'

Rita saw the sense in what he had said. Although she agreed to end the relationship, she was unwilling to part away with him just like that. So she planned and successfully lured him into making love to her over and she hoped to do it over and over again. Charles' constant need to make love to a woman made it easy for her to succeed. The tactful method of luring him proved it to Charles that she was not a novice. She was, as a matter of fact an expert love game player.

He could not stop the game as he expected for the mere fact that he was always sexually starved. He found Rita so pleasant and sexually satisfying that she needed not to play any trick before she lured him to the bed. All she needed to do was to create the environment they could be alone where she could uncover her seducing body and allow him to see what he was missing in a woman.

Before people got to know about the affairs, however, he had successfully put an end to the relationship with Rita and switched to her friend called Marie who sometimes rode with them when they were going to their offices.

Before Rita knew that Charles was dating Marie, their love had gone to the advance stage - a point of no return.

\

FOUR

Marie worked in the same office with Rita. She was so outstandingly beautiful that Charles who believed he could not be easily lured into any relationship found himself secretly admiring her the first day Rita introduced her to him as her friend and co-worker. Since the time Charles set his eyes on her, he had been very helpful to the two ladies. He always took them to the office nearly everyday. Anytime he was not available to give them the usual ride, he would give them some money to chatter a taxi.

While returning from the office one day, Charles told his driver to take the route to Marie's house before going back home. Even though that was not the usual practice, Rita did not suspect that Charles plan to find out where Marie lived so that he would go to her and declare his intention to make her his lover.

About a week later, Charles paid Marie an unexpected visit.

Marie felt highly honoured when she saw him. She gave him a VIP treatment. Although She suspected that he was interested in her through the way he treated her and Rita, she didn't expect a man of his high status to pay her a visit for the fun of it. She, however, decided to play the simple and ignorant.

'You know, Marie,' Charles began in a soft sweet tongue; trying to recall how he talked his wife into relationship about twenty years before, 'you're a very beautiful lady.'

Looking away, she replied, 'well... I don't really know.'

'I'm telling you that you are,' he said, smiling at her and getting carried away by her charm.

There was a long silence which Marie found uncomfortable. She was anxious to know his deep feelings but she kept her peace.

'You know I'm married?' he asked.

She nodded slowly and almost sadly as if she was aware of what he was going through in his marriage.

'Well,' he continued gently. 'There's one thing missing in my marriage. That thing is breaking my heart into two. My wife is having the lion share of my broken heart. I reserve the other share for the lady that would offer me romance. Romance is what is missing in my

51

marriage. If not, I would not have had the mind to have extra-marital affair with anyone. I love my wife and children very much but my wife hates romance. I need someone to give me romance. Would you give it to me?' He looked at her. She was not looking at him.

She sighed after a moment. 'You request me to give you romance,' she said, 'how can I give it to you when you have not even said you love me. Romance is not all that makes love. There are other things too. You know, I'm not a prostitute. So I cannot give you romance for anything else except for the sake of love.'

'Actually, Marie,' he said, 'I love you.'

'Why didn't you say that in the first place?' she questioned. 'That will make more sense to me than just telling me about romance.'

'The reason I didn't say I love you is that you might not believe me. I mean how can a married man come to you and say "I love you" when you're fully aware that he'll not marry you.'

'Well-em,' she said, looking thoughtful. 'I don't know what to say actually.'

'Just tell me how you feel about me. We'll think of how things will work out later.'

'Sincerely speaking, I love you too. I love your virtues and many other things about you,' she said. 'But you know I'm twenty-five and very soon, I'll be thinking of having a husband. What happens to our romance when I get married?'

'Let's wait till then,' Charles said.

She shrugged and said, 'okay.'

'Get some wine and let's drink over this new found love.'

She went to the kitchen to get a bottle of wine and two glass cups. She took them to him. He opened the bottle, poured it inside the cups. They drank the wine and soon began to chat, caressed each other and then eventually made love in her bedroom.

******

Marie lived with her elder brother when her relationship with Charles began. Her brother who was called Femi was a medical doctor. When he discovered the relationship, he was the first person to kick against it.

'I don't expect someone of your age to get involved with a married man,' Femi said. 'Isn't there any other man in the town for you to get hooked with except married man?'

'I love Charles,' Marie said firmly. 'Nothing can change that.'

'It is better you're sincere with yourself,' Femi said. 'You're not really in love with him. You're in love with his money.'

The disagreement between the two of them caused Marie to start looking for another place to live.

Charles later got to know Femi's wife through his daughter who was her junior when they were in secondary school. Femi too got to know Charles but his response to his greetings proved that he would stop at nothing but to ruin his relationship with his sister.

The love between Marie and Charles became so strong that they could no longer hide it even from Funke. Many people began to anticipate that Charles would either turn his family to polygamy or kick his wife out of the house. Charles was unwilling to do either. After getting Marie an accommodation, he began to take care of her. He furnished the house and bought her many things.

About two months later Marie became pregnant. Since many people including his family already knew about the relationship, he registered her at a very prestigious hospital for the antenatal treatment. Her maiden surname was replaced with his surname. The implication of that was that she was already becoming his second wife even though he was yet to be fully aware of it.

The proprietor and chief medical director of the hospital were Charles' close friends. So Marie had all the attention of the specialist doctors she needed. When she fell into labour seven months later, she was taken to the hospital. The chief medical director was contacted at home. Within some minutes, he was already at the hospital. Around this time, Charles was out of the town on official duty. The chief medical director personally undertook the delivery of the child. After several hours of labour, she delivered a baby boy but, to the doctor's sorrow; it was a still birth. Nobody could explain what caused of the child's death. There was no complication and there was no mistake on the part of the doctor. In fact, the baby was alive almost through out the labour. The doctor concluded that this was probably the finger of God or perhaps the devil that did not want the child to live.

When Charles returned from the official tour, he was told of what happened. The incident really beat his imagination. What caused the death of the baby after all the medical attentions the mother had been getting right from the time she was taken to the hospital for antenatal treatment? But there was one simple answer to it, as he could perceive it. He was going against the pledges he had made to God and Funke by getting so much involved with Marie.

He went to sit under a tree to think about his life. He thought of where things went wrong and who was responsible. He thought of the covenant he made with God on the issue of marriage when he was thirteen years old. He had violated nearly everything he had pledged. But then could he really blame himself for all the wrongs he has done? He has married Funke with the hope that she would give him all the benefits and pleasures of marriage but her weak sexual urge and inability to accommodate his sexual demand had frustrated him, forcing him into having extramarital affairs with other women. If he had known that Funke was not as romantic as he thought, he would probably not have made such promises.

After looking at the situation very critically, he decided to take Marie his second wife so as to give her the second chance to give birth. Of course, he knew that adultery was a sin, let alone marrying two wives but he cared less about it. After all, he had no choice but to marry again if he really did not want to jump around with women again.

He went to Marie at home to tell her what he has in mind.

As soon as she saw his expression, she knew that something that might change the trend of her life was about to happen.

'Marie,' he said softly. 'I've known you for years now. I know you to be a faithful, caring and loving lady.' He went on. 'You filled the vacuum in my life and I want that vacuum filled permanently. I therefore want you be my second wife subject to four conditions.'

Marie asked as softly as he had been addressing her, 'what are the conditions?' Already she had made up her mind to accept all the conditions even if they were not convenient.

'The conditions are: the marriage between us will be on mutual understanding without official registration in the marriage registry or church since I cannot divorce Funke.

'Secondly, we will not live together as husband and wife under the same roof. Instead I will provide a very suitable accommodation for you outside my matrimonial home. I will take good care of you and the children you give me.

'Also, you will be introduced only to my immediate family members. And lastly you must give Funke the maximum respect accorded to a mother at all times. You must not disrespect her for any reason otherwise the relationship will be terminated immediately.' He paused to look at her. 'Do you accept these conditions?'

Without hesitating, Marie said, 'I do.'

Later Charles talked to Funke about the proposal. She always cooperated with him in virtually everything. In fact, she kept most of the promises she made to Charles. The only area which she did not meet up to his expectation was the expression of her love through sex.

Charles explained that he merely wanted Marie to make up for her weakness and that she was the only legal wife. If she could permit him to marry Marie, she would no longer hear reports of his involvement with ladies.

'You're sure that the stability of this family will not be threatened by another family you are setting up outside?'

'I promise you it'll not.'

'No woman would love to have a rival, you know,' Funke said, 'but you may do what you wish.'

With that response from Funke, Charles married Marie unofficially. The marriage was celebrated in her sitting room with few friends and relatives.

FIVE

For the period of eleven years, Charles had no cause to be involved with any lady except his two wives. Marie satisfied him sexually even though she didn't bear any child as they anticipated. She, however, suddenly became a jealous woman; probably because she suspected that Charles would soon kick her out and replace her with another lady. She fought every lady she suspected to be in love with him. As Charles was naturally endowed with many good qualities, he was very much loved by many people including his employees. Marie fought some of the ladies that worked with him. She at times caused them to loose their jobs. Marie's behaviour soon became an embarrassment to Charles.

'I'm very much in love with you,' he told her one day. 'And you always satisfy me sexually. Why then should I flirt around with any other lady? You know I'm very faithful to you, Marie.'

'I don't believe you!' she screamed at him. 'I'm a lady. So I know what an amorous stare is. I've seen those ladies goggling at you.'

'Why don't you believe me?' Charles said, glowering at her. "And save both of us from unnecessary embarrassment?'

Charles who had previously gotten her a job in his company decided to withdraw her and made her a full time housewife so that she could follow him whenever he went round the country, touring. That gave her the opportunity to keep watch over him as she liked. He gave her the freedom to monitor him as she liked with the hope that it would prove his innocence and faithfulness. She could not find anything against him but she often listened to some malicious rumours that were intended by her friends to pull them apart. She never knew that these friends were jealous of her position as the wife of the chairman and managing director for such a big organization. So they planned to ruin her peace with him by fabricating stories that Charles was always having secret affairs with some ladies in all the places he toured. Marie believed every story she heard. This always resulted into quarrel and arguments between him and the innocent ladies.

'I'm tired of all these nonsense!' Charles bellowed at her one day

56

after she accused him of going to a meeting with a lady. 'Can't you for a moment give me a rest? You're always nagging and complaining about ladies that meant nothing to me.'

'Well, I'll not stand by and look at someone plucking out my eyes.'

'Nobody wants to pull out your eyes, you this foolish woman. It is you who is causing problem for yourself by listening to those who gossip about me going after women,' Charles said angrily. 'You don't have to help the people who are jealous of you to pull down your home.'

'You lied, you know,' Marie said. 'Nobody is jealous of me. Why should they be jealous? I don't have any child. Other women threaten to give you children if I don't chase them away from you.'

There was a lady who was his correspondence officer. She was tall, dark and beautiful. She was elegant and very attractive. Marie was worried about her appearance. She believed the lady normally dressed to entice Charles. To Marie, it was a lot easy for him to take her into his office and make love to her.

'That lady,' Marie challenged him one day, 'is having an affair with you.'

'What?' Charles could not believe her blind jealousy. 'She's my correspondence officer.'

'So what!' she screamed, mad with jealousy. 'You could have had a man to do the job but you chose her because of the occasional fun you normally have with her.'

'What?' He found it hard to believe she said that. 'Did you hear yourself, Marie? You really believe that I'm so irresponsible that I can do a thing like that in the office?'

'Why not?' she shot at him in anger. 'Every lady who is close to you knows that you've always enjoy sex anywhere.'

He looked more dumbfounded.

'Proof me wrong if you can!'

'You're insane,' he told her firmly.

'Insane? Am I?' she asked. 'You've always wanted a beautiful lady around you all the time in case to you want to have some fun. That's the reason you employ the lady. You could have had an ugly woman to do the job of your clerk even if you don't want a man but you chose a beautiful - cute lady.'

'You seriously need help, Marie. You better go and see a psychiatrist.'

'If there is anyone that needs help, it's you. You need to do something about your uncontrollable sexual urge that makes you flirt

57

around wit every lady you see.'

Charles could not find anything to say for a long time. He looked at her with self pity, wondering at the way she reasoned. He concluded at that moment that jealousy was capable of making a person to loose his or her sanity. After a while, he said with all sincerity; 'believe me you urgently need to see a psychiatrist.'

'Now say something that'll prove me wrong,' she said.

'You've gone out of your mind, Marie,' he said. 'That's all I can say.'

The following day, Marie stormed his office and beat the correspondent officer senselessly. The lady could not even lift her hand back at her because of the deep respect she has for Charles.

When Charles returned to the office, he was told what Marie has done.

'I wish you're around to witness what Madam did,' his secretary told him. 'She turned the office into a battlefield. She really d sgraced the officer. In fact, I don't know how to explain it. Because the officer never lifted her hand against her, Madam had the chance to beat her like that. I have to ask her to take the day off to treat herself in the hospital.'

Charles felt disgraced and frustrated. He went slowly to his office and threw himself heavily on the chair. He was now at the peak of the frustration in his life. For the first time in his life, he regretted having falling into the ocean of love with two women who neither seemed ready to give him all the joy, peace and benefit he had been seeking for in his marriage. Something was wrong with his life, he thought. If he had not had an insight into other people's marriages, he would have thought that there could never be any joy in getting married. Funke was loving, understanding and co-operative but she was too weak for him sexually. Now that he had opted for Marie to make up for her weakness, another problem showed its ugly face. There was no feeling that was as bad as blind jealousy. It has turned a once loving woman into something he could rightly called a bitch. He had tried all he could to erase that the feelings of jealousy in Marie but it seemed to him that nothing could remove it. The only way he could be free from the problem she was giving him was to do away with her. But then, doing away with her would mean two things. He would go back to his original position of unromantic life unless he picked another lady. Secondly, it would appear as if he had used Marie like a tissue paper after spending about twelve years of her life meeting his sexual needs. He was in a dilemma.

Charles who was naturally humble and loving went to thank all the employees who had settled the fight. That day, he went to the correspondence officer's house to tender his long apology.

'I'm the one that offended you,' he told her. 'So I want you to please, forgive me.'

'Oh, sir,' the lady said modestly, 'I've already forgiven her even before you ask me to.' She was very sincere with what she had said. She did not forgive Marie for causing her the greatest embarrassment of her life because she was her employer's wife but because she was very fond of Charles. Charles was one of the most virtuous persons she had ever met. In fact, she secretly adored him for all his virtues. She could not hide this from him in the way she related with him in the office. Perhaps that was what gave Marie the wrong impression that she was in love with him. She truly loved Charles but not in the way she thought. Charles was old enough to be her father. So to her, being in love with him as Marie thought was a great misconception.

Charles gave the lady some money to take care of herself before he left. The money was so much that she knelt down and thanked him wholeheartedly.

At home, Charles tried to correct Marie and make her see her folly hut she reacted violently. Only the age difference between them held her from fighting him physically.'

'At your age,' she stormed, 'you are still playing hanky-panky with a lady of your daughter's age.'

'Marie,' Charles got annoyed, glaring at her, 'how can you in your right senses imagine such evil? You are a disgrace to me!'

'Who is a disgrace to whom?' she asked with fury. 'I tell you you're not only a disgrace to yourself and me but to the class of people you represent in the society. I can not imagine someone of your caliber descending so low as to be jumping and flirting around with your clerk! Clerk! Shame!'

The root of Marie's jealousy could not be traced nor understood. It was as if she had hidden these traits at the early stage of their relationship. One thing was inevitable to Charles, however, she would either change or leave him for another man. Otherwise, she would drive him out of his mind. As the adage says, there is limit to human endurance. Funke, his real wife did not him so much problem. How could he continue to endure the lady who has no other job except to pester his life and make every minute of his life miserable?

Charles deliberately stayed away from her for weeks, paying unnecessary visits to all the branches of his company. Funke and the children were so used to his constant absence from home that it didn't

59

make much difference to them if he was around or not. Although she would have preferred him to be at home all the time, she knew it was her weakness that had made her to share him with another woman. It was really insane, some of her friends and relatives once told her when they leant about the second marriage. One of her friends pointed out that if not for the good virtues in Charles, her marriage would have gone into history.

'Your husband,' one of her friends had pointed out, 'is a rare man. In spite of you denying him the very essential part of marriage, he is still able to keep the family together.'

All what her friends and relatives said made her accept the situation as it was.

One Sunday, while Charles was in another state; still trying to find a place to hide from Marie who has now become a constant source of sorrow to him, he went to a church where his life took a different dimension. The Pastor of the church delivered a powerful sermon as if someone has narrated what Charles was going through to him.

'I read the book of Hosea chapter four from verse one to you. It says, "hear the word of the Lord, you children of Israel: for the Lord has a controversy with the inhabitants of the land, because there is no truth, nor mercy, nor knowledge of God in the land.

'"By swearing and lying, and killing, and stealing, and committing adultery, they break all restraint, with bloodshed upon bloodshed."

'I read verse six, "My people are destroyed for lack of knowledge: because you have rejected knowledge, I will also reject you that thou shall be no priest to Me; Because you have forgotten the law of your God, I will also forget thy children.

'"As they were increased, so they sinned against me: therefore will I change their glory into shame."'

He looked at the people as they stared at him expectantly. 'I will title my message as "destruction for lack of knowledge." I will first of all give you this illustration before I begin the message.

'There was an American who came to Nigeria for a research. He was a doctor who wanted to know the cause of a certain disease in Africa. He has a girlfriend who got pregnant. This doctor decided to carry out an abortion on the lady. In the process of doing that, the doctor was caught and charged for the offence of abortion. He pleaded that he didn't know that abortion was illegal in Nigeria. Down in his country, abortion was not illegal. The doctor was convicted on the ground that ignorance of the law is not an excuse to break the law.

'Destruction for lack of knowledge is common everywhere. Even

60

in the Christendom. From the passage we read in the Bible, the word of God says; "hear the word of the Lord, you children of Israel: for the Lord has a controversy with the inhabitants of the land." When you hear the word of God, it must influence your life. When you hear the word of God, you must accept it. When you accept the word of God, it must change your entire life. But it's a pity many heard the word of God, it never move them because they don't believe it. Some believed it but they never apply it into their lives.

'The Lord had controversy with the people of the land because there's no truth, no mercy and no knowledge of God in the land. So they swear, they tell lies, they steal, they commit adultery and they are involved in all kinds of evil that offend God. It doesn't matter to them if their Maker was angry at them or not. Sins became the order of the day. Sins are part of the norms of the land. The preacher would not tell them the truths because they are afraid of losing their meals or lives.

'The Bible says in verse three of that passage: "the land shall mourn, and everyone that dwells in the bondage of sin shall languish! You that live your life anyhow, you shall account for that life. You shall see where you will end up on the judgment day. Although people may see you as a nice, loving or kind man but on that day every little sin in your life shall be revealed and that blemish will send you to hell. I pray that no one of you will be with any blemish in Jesus' name."

'Amen,' the people replied.

'You thief that think no one see you when you take other people's things shall see yourself on that day. You whoremonger - adulterer and fornicator shall see yourself as you sneaked with that man or woman into the hotel on that day. And you'll see hell opening its mouth to receive you.

'There was a very strange event I heard on the radio sometimes ago about a woman whose husband resides in a town while she and the children lived in another town. The husband normally went to visit the family every weekend. The woman took the advantage of' her husband's absence to develop a relationship with another man. Her lover normally went to sleep with her in the house while the husband was not in the town. This woman gave birth to three children or so. Then one day, the lover told the woman, "well, I think you know that I am the father of these children. So I need them now." There was an argument between them but they later agreed to get rid of the husband through a charm called magun. How it works was simple. The spirit in the charm would be invoked into the woman and stay there for seven days after which she would die if no one made love

61

with her. If any man made love with her within those days, he would kick the bucket after taken a certain type of food or so. The woman allowed the spirit to be invoked into her and then waited for her husband to enter into the trap. The plan was that when the man died, the lover would become her full husband and father of the children. 'As usual, the husband came to see his family on weekend but as God will have it, the moment he got into the house, he began to feel funny. He was quite alright when he left the town where he worked but he would not understand why he was feeling feverish the moment he stepped into the house.

'Knowing what it means for the husband to fall sick at that time, she tried to make him feel better by getting him some drugs. The fever never left the man. At night, the woman tried in vain to seduce him. Throughout the weekend, the man did not make love to the woman until he went back.

'Now the woman knew she was in a big trouble. She has just three days to persuade a man to make love to her or get ready to die. Who wants to die? was the question the commentator asked. Of course, the woman was unwilling to die. So she went to her lover who eagerly asked her if her husband has struck the trap. She assured him that he had struck it. He was convinced that the spirit must have left the woman. So he climbed on top of her and struck the trap. The man later died. The woman was compelled by her conscience to reveal what had happened to her husband. The husband who was as surprised as anyone that hears this story threw it open into the air.

'Now listen!' the preacher exclaimed. 'There are so many atrocities going around the world. The sins in this world are far greater than the sins of Sodom and Gomorrah. Why? It is because there's no truth. Some people out of their selfish and lustful desire will cheat on their spouses. Perhaps you don't know that God gives you only a man or a woman to marry. If you marry more than one wife or husband, you're an adulterer. Some married people caused their spouses to go into adultery by denying them sexual needs. Let me tell you one thing, if that man or woman does not make heaven, God will require his or her soul from you.

'Truth is hardly preached everywhere. That's why people do what they like.

'In verse six of the passage, the Lord says. "My people are destroyed for lack of knowledge." It goes on to say they don't have knowledge because they have rejected it. God says He will reject anyone that rejects knowledge.

'Many people run about, looking for peace. They cannot stay with their nagging wives or their intolerant husbands because they don't have knowledge. When you see your husband or wife as a bad man or woman after spending several years together, it means there's something wrong with you too. Even the devil as wicked as he is was permitted to relate with God. God tolerated him. Do I see somebody in disagreement with me? Alright, I'll prove it to you in the Bible. Open to the book of Job chapter one from verse six. I'll read just few verses to you. When you get home, you can go and read the rest.

'"Now there was a day when the sons of God came to present themselves before the Lord, and Satan came also among them.

'"And the Lord said unto Satan, whence comest thou? Then Satan answered the Lord, and said from going to and fro in the earth, and from walking up and down in it."'

He looked at the people. 'When you read the whole chapter, you'll see that Satan relates with God as if they are not enemies. He had an argument with God about Job which was resolved when God allowed him to do whatever he liked with Job except touching his life.

'You can pause for a while and think about it. God was talking to Satan after what he tried to do to Him in heaven. Although God still plans to deal with Satan for what he did, He never allowed that to influence Him in the way He relates with him. You see here that, as a child of God with God's image and characteristics, we should be able to tolerate one another. Some Christians cannot tolerate each other let alone to tolerate their enemies. And yet Jesus says we should love our enemies. Just because there's difference in your opinion and that of your fellow human beings does not mean you should not relate with him. There is no good relationship in some homes, no family altar - nothing except "good morning." After greetings, no one cares who or how the family members survived. Love is lacking in many people's hearts. They love with mouths and not with their hearts. That's why things go wrong. Love is a very thick chain that binds people together...'

The preacher's sermon began to get more and more powerful until Charles could no longer resist his emotional feelings. He covered his face and wept softly. He whispered, 'Oh Lord, forgive me. I've been wrong all my life and I did not even know it. Teach me what to do and I promise you I'll follow you for the rest of my life.'

63

SIX

When Charles returned home, he was told that Marie hac packed out of the town. She told people she was fed up with Charles. Charles went on his kneels in his room and began to thank God. He knew that God was putting many things in order in his life.

He went to his family. Funke was the first to welcome him home. For the first time in years, she smiled whole heartedly at him. She held his hand and led him to the dinning table. Dumbly, he sat at the dinning table; wondering what in the whole wide world was happening.

Funke called all the children who were now grown up and went to the kitchen to get the cake she has baked. It was as they expected him to come that day. The children made the table, putting plates of delicious chicken, rice and other food in front of their father.

Still unable to comprehend what was happening, Charles continued to look at his family presenting what look like drama.

Funke put her chair besides his, smiling at him. The eldest child stood up to address everybody.

'Well,' he said, looking formal, 'I'm glad to inform every member of this family that daddy and mummy are wedding again.'

Everybody except Charles who was rather baffled cheered, clapping happily.

Almost tearfully, the eldest child continued as if he understood what his father had been going through, 'Jesus set up this family and nobody - I say nobody can tear it apart.'

The rest shouted, 'yes '

'We'll not allow any other woman to take our father from our mother!'

'Yeah!'

Tears ran down Funke's eyes. She knew it was all her fault. God gave her a good husband who did all he could to make her and the children happy. She had hurt him and wounded every good thing in him. She did not give what it took to keep her family together. She did not make the sacrifice it required to keep him. She made him an irresponsible man that flirted around with ladies and turned him into bigamist. She knew her husband was the kind of man any sane

64

woman would do anything to keep. The children knew that their father was a very virtuous man and everybody knew that he did not deserve the way she had been treating him. Now that she knew that it was all her fault, she was ready and determined to give all she could, including her life to make him happy and make up for what he had gone through.

'Mummy, tell daddy you love him,' the eldest child was saying.

'I love you,' she whispered

'Daddy,' the young man continued, 'we know you love us and mummy because love is best expressed in conduct. We know through the way you've always cared for us that you love us. Still, I want you to tell us you love us.'

It was becoming impossible for Charles not to cry with both joy and great love for his family. But he managed to say in a shaky voice. 'I love you all.'

'Now, cut the cake together to prove it to us as I count three.'

Charles quickly held the knife in the cake with Funke.

'One...' he said. 'Two... three...'

They cut the cake and all the children clapped their hands. Charles cut two pieces and put one into Funke's mouth. Funke took the other and did likewise.

Funke pulled Charles' hand. 'Come on, let's go to the bed room for honeymoon.'

They got into the room and Funke for the first time demanded that Charles should make love to her. They made love. Charles felt so happy that he wept. Funke was so moved as well that she burst out sobbing. She said within her sobs, 'I'm sorry for all I have done to you over the years. The Lord just opened my eyes through our children that I was the one tearing the family apart. I promise you to be as romantic as possible.'

'And I promise to have only you as my wife,' he said.

Since that day, the family became a very adorable set. Charles has no cause to have another wife since Funke changed. Besides every one of them has become a Christian.

THE RUNAWAY WIFE

ONE

I just finished writing the story titled "The genesis of love" which was to be serialized in the Sunday Tribune in Nigeria in the year 1995 and decided to take a stroll to my friend's house down the street. Victor, my friend was my course mate at the Polytechnic, although he was older than me. We were both civil servants then, running diploma programs on part time. We were both poorly paid but he managed to get a financial breakthrough through the source which I cannot explain. He has a big bungalow and a very beautiful car. Some people were of the opinion that he made his money through the football team that was run by the government establishment where he worked while some said he must have looted part of the public funds that were meant to run the establishment. I wouldn't like to believe either of the stories for the mere fact that there was no proof of all the allegations. Since many could be jealous of success of other people, I did not border to find out how he made his money. I must confess, however, that for a poorly paid civil servant like Victor to be rich enough to build a grand house and buy a car like that was questionable at the time of economic crisis in the country. Wherever he got his money from, I really did not care to know. All I knew was that I owed him the word of God and that was what we normally shared each time we were together.

I met Victor sitting down on the low fence of his house, looking so downcast that I sensed it that he must have been crying. Throughout the three years we spent together in the school, I never saw him feeling so unhappy; let alone looking as if he would cry. He was always a happy guy. In fact, when things seemed to be going pretty tough for most people, making them to hang their problems on their faces, he was always a happy-go-lucky guy that has nothing to worry about.

Feeling concerned, I quickly went to join him where he was sitting and asked, 'Brother Victor, what's wrong?'

'Pastor Toby,' he said with deep regrets. 'As you see me, I am a dead person. My life is ruined.'

Trying to console him with some jokes, I said, 'I don't think you know the man whose life is ruined and in case you don't know who a dead man is, let me take you to the mortuary.'

'If I tell you what happened to me,' he said, 'you'll understand what I mean.'

'Okay,' I said. 'Tell me what happened.'

He gave a deep sigh of sorrow before he began. 'Long before now, I observed that my wife had been going to a white garment church. Even then, I didn't feel any qualm about that. Apart from going to the church, I also observed that she bought a lot of expensive things which my annual income could not purchase. I've caught her smelling and looking drunk on many occasions. Really, all these didn't border me much. What I was bordered about was her carefree attitudes towards my two kids. You know, those children mean so much to me. I always take the pain to bath and dress them before taking them to the school. I even cooked the food if their mother did not wake up on time.

'I called her one day and complained about her attitude but she got furious at me. You know I'm a peace loving man. So I left her alone. I don't want people coming into my house to settle quarrel. I learned not to complain about her attitude, hoping that she will change.

'When she started going to this white garment church. I thought she'll change but I was wrong. In fact, she got worse. She kept buying more expensive things and before I knew it, she was deep in adultery. Not every man can stand another man sleeping with his wife. You know, I could have kicked her out of my house but for my love for her. Besides, if I send her out, will I bring in another woman to be the mother of my two children? More so, how could I tell if the next woman will not be worse?

'I decided to talk to her about it. I told her how she could ruin her family with the way she was behaving. I asked her if she could stand seeing me with another lady. Instead of her to use the same soft tone with which I was addressing her, she flared up and began to rain obscenities on me. I could not stand it any longer. I got angry at her and told her that if she was going to the church of godly people, she wouldn't be acting like that. Guess what happened, she told the people in the church what I said. I'm sure she would have exaggerated what I said. Before long, someone informed me that the people in the church saw the wrong vision that I was planning to kill her by poisoning her food and then marry another lady. The next thing I observed was that she started burning candles at every nook and cranny of the room. Not only that, anytime I prepared the food in the house, she would not eat it. She would complain that she didn't like the way 1 cooked the food or she would say she didn't feel like eating. All these continued for a long time until one day when the unexpected happened.

'I went to my office where one of my friends confronted me with a puzzling question. He asked me why I wanted to sell my car and my house. I told him I didn't plan to sell anything. He asked me why I was telling people to come and buy the car and the house. I could not understand what was happening. It was after I met the man that I understood what was happening. My wife has gone to tell many people that I was planning to travel out of the country. So I needed money for the flight tickets. In order to raise the money, I needed to sell all my properties. In fact the house and the car would have been sold if my wife had laid hold on the papers. If not for God that led me to keep all the documents, which my wife needed to dispose all the properties, I would have become homeless destitute by now.'

I was stunned to discover what my wife was trying to do without knowing that a bigger surprise awaited me at home. My wife has disposed everything I have in the house including my cloths, hired a lorry and carted everything she felt was useful to her. The real nail in my coffin was my children whom she took with her.'

Suddenly he burst out crying like a baby.

Emotion engulfed me. I felt so sorry for him that I felt like crying too. But then, I knew I must not show how much I pitied him if I really wanted to help him. I controlled my emotion even though it was so heart breaking to think of innocent children falling into the hand of a woman like that.

I prayed inwardly to God for the right words.

I stared at him for a moment before I began, 'do you believe you're the cause of your own problem?'

He stared back at me and asked, 'how?'

'You might find this strange,' I said. 'But let's look at it in my own way and in the way of God. The Bible says in the book of proverb chapter 28 verse 18 that whosoever walk uprightly shall be saved; but he that is perverse in his ways shall fall at once.' I paused to allow him digest the passage. 'You see, when something goes wrong in the life of a man, he tends to find someone to blame. He blames his wife, he blames his parents, he blames everybody but he never sits down and thinks of the foundation of his life. You may think you have a bad wife but I have to tell you the problem is not with your wife. It is, as a matter of fact, with you. You did not build your home on a solid ground. As the old adage says, the dew shall demolish the house that is built with saliva. You built your home on the wrong foundation because you lack

69

knowledge of the word of God. The Bible says in the book of Hosea chapter 4 verse 6 that the people of God perish because they lack knowledge. What is the knowledge I'm talking about? You may ask. It is the knowledge about God. The first thing you're supposed to know when you're born is Jesus Christ because He is the Author of life. When you have knowledge of Jesus Christ, it is then you have someone to guide you in every step you take in life. I am not saying your wife is not to be blamed. What I'm saying is that both of you have wrong foundations. If you are to blame her for what she has done to you. I'm sure there's someone out there who will blame you too for what you have done to hurt him. I don't know whom you have hurt but I know you have hurt someone since your life began. If you feel your wife owes you an apology, you also owe that person an apology. At least, we all owe God an apology for all we have done to him because the Bible says we have all sinned. Before anything can be put right in your life, you need to be born-again. Otherwise, you'll not have peace in your life and in your family.

'I want you to commit your life and family into the hand of God and let's see how he would put them in order. Do you want to do that?'

He nodded.

'Let's pray then,' I said. We closed our eyes, holding each other's hands and then prayed. From his reaction, I could perceive that he sincerely wanted to dedicate his life to Christ.

The following day, we tried to locate Victor's wife who was called Sarah through her close friends. Our preliminary investigations revealed that Sarah has gone to the northern part of the country. This almost broke Victor's heart. His great concern was the children she had taken with her. He thought she was a very careless mother who would not take proper care of the children. If only he could get his children back, he lamented, he wouldn't have to go through any trouble trying to find her.

He applied for his annual leave in the office and traveled down to the north while I prayed with him in the south. He spent the whole leave in the north without even getting a trace of his family. He went to many people including his wife's aunty whom he expected to at least know her whereabouts but none of them could tell where she was. Although he was not sure if they were telling him the truth, he had no cause to tell anyone of them this. All he could say as an appeal to them was, 'I just want to see my children.' His wife, he told me later, could choose to go to blazes for all he cared.

He came back to the south more dejected than ever. I tried to console him but all he wanted were his children. I knew he must have spent quite a fortune while looking for his family so I felt obliged to give him the little money I could offer just to encourage him in the search for his family.

I organized prayer group in the Church to start interceding on behalf of the family. I knew it was the devil attacking the family. If not, I did not see how a sane woman who was quite comfortable with her husband to be influenced by some demonic people who covered their filth with white garment to pack out of the house. I knew so much about the white garment churches that I was not surprised that they could break homes. Often times, when I shared my knowledge about certain churches, many people would think I was just criticizing them for the fun of it without realizing that I was only trying to let them see the difference between the church of God and that of the evil people that pose as children of God. Right in the church of evil people, I have seen the leader making love with the wife of another man. They could exhibit the counterfeit gifts, bring about miracles and healing and even speak in tongues that are attributed to demons. They could prophesy with the influence of evil spirits and give vivid picture of what has happened to someone in the past just to convince that person they are using the power of God. Strange enough, the followers were always convinced that the churches were using the power of God. Once they were convinced that the power of God was in the church, the people began to do whatever the leader told them to do. Even when the leader committed unimaginable piles of atrocities, they never question him. It was really a great deception. A person could have his or her problem solved by simply coming to sleep in the church, which were sometimes built beside water - a place that was ideal for demonic operations.

Many years ago, my mother was compelled to go to the church because of the financial problem in my family. She could no longer cope with the situation in the family. So she went to seek for solution in the church. At that time I didn't know so much about God. My mother was told to sweep the church for seven days after which she would begin to experience changes in the family's financial condition. Perhaps the leader of the church either guessed that my mother was not likely to accept the idea of coming to sleep in the church for those days or he would have preferred a younger lady to do that.

For seven days, my mother would wake up at dawn to go and sweep the church. After sweeping the church for those days, nothing improved in my family as she anticipated. In fact, it was right after then that I lost my father and things fell apart. What a solution! I guess it was the same solution that was offered to Victor's family.

After I have organized the group of people, we began serious prayer; breaking all the curses the people might have put upon the family and rendering all the powers of darkness useless.

Four months later, God began to answer our prayer for Victor's family. Of course, we never gave up praying.

Victor's children were seen going to a school in one neighboring town by his co-worker who was transferred to the place lately. John, the co-worker was not even aware that Victor had been looking for the children. He called and asked them about their father. Dotun, the older of the children told him they have not seen their father for almost five months.

John looked interested. He began to interrogate her. 'What happened?'

Dotun began to tell him what happened. She said 'we are supposed to be going to school on that day when my mother told me and my brother that we would be leaving the house for another place. She said we should wait in the house. She went to get a big lorry. She and some men began to pack everything in the house. I told her that I'm not going but she beat me. So I had to follow her.'

'Did your father know when you left?' John asked.

'No,' she replied quickly. 'If he had known, he wouldn't have allowed her to take us away.'

John looked puzzled. 'Didn't he look for you?'

'I don't know,' she replied. 'Do you know where he is, sir? I want to see him.' Then the poor girl began to cry.

'You will surely see him,' John assured her, 'because I'm going to tell him I saw you.' He looked at her younger brother called Seun who was silent and then stared back at Dotun. 'Where do you live now?'

'I...don't know what the place is called,' she replied. 'It's a big house beside Lola supermarket.'

'How do you know Lola supermarket,' John asked, 'and yet you don't know where you live?'

'Daddy used to take us there to buy gifts for us. He used to tell us about the place.'

'Which daddy?' John asked, guessing right that their mother must have taken the children to live with another man.

'The one at home,' Dotun said innocently. 'He used to take care of us like our real daddy.'

'Do you want to see your real daddy?' John asked.

'Yes,' the children replied quickly.

'Now, if you want to see your real daddy, you must not tell your mother what happened now. Do you understand?'

The children nodded.

'If you tell her,' John continued, 'she will take you away and your daddy will not reach you again.'

'We'll not tell her,'

'Don't tell anybody, do you understand?'

They nodded.

'By this time tomorrow when going to school, your daddy will wait for you here.'

'Yippee!' the children looked happy and ran towards their school.

John went to his office and called Victor on the phone to inform him about his children. He became so frantic that he would have dashed down to the town that day if not that John told him that he was not likely to see them. If not for the delay, Victor would not have come to inform me of what he was planning to do and if he had not come, he would have probably taken the wrong step.

'You mean you'll go to the town and arrest your wife and the man she's living with?' I asked.

'Yes,' he replied. 'In fact I have informed a police friend that will help me carry out my intention before coming here.'

'You don't mean that, do you?'

'I mean it!' he shouted. 'The wicked woman had tortured me long enough. It's about time I take my revenge.

'God says, "vengeance is mine,"' I said. 'So you cannot take any revenge. Besides, do you imagine that the kids were found through your efforts? You have tried all your efforts but failed. Now that God had helped you find them, you want to leave Him aside and use your initiative to take action.'

'So what do you suggest I do now?' he asked almost scornfully. 'Leave the Jezebel alone so she could continue to torture me till I die?'

'She's still your wife,' I reminded him. 'If you don't recognize that, God and the law still recognize it.'

'You really think I can still put that wicked and cheap whore under my roof?'

'Hey, come on, I said. 'The Bible says we wrestle not against flesh and blood but against principalities and powers.'

'What has that got to do with my children and the prostitute of a wife?' he asked, getting irritated.

'Can't you understand?' I asked. 'Can't you understand that

there's a force controlling her? I mean she was not created to be what she is. She was created to be a child of God. You must not condemn her because she can still change. Anybody can change. I know it's difficult to accept this but she can be a prodigal wife who will still come back to you.'

'Come back to me?' he spat. 'You think I'll be crazy to take her back? The marriage is over. We're going to get a divorce and I'm going to get another woman.'

'God hates divorce. You are not going to do what God hates after helping you to locate your children. If she comes back, you'll have to accept her,' I told him. 'That's the principle of God and we have to accept it that way. The father of the prodigal son never sent him away when he went back to him.'

'You know,' he said, 'at times I find you too fanatical for my liking.'

I was silent, a little bit hurt.

He quickly sensed my feelings. He said gently, 'I'm sorry. I know you're only concerned. You have helped in so many ways. I'm sorry.'

'It's okay,' I said, smiling at him.

'You cannot make me take more than what I can chew,' he said. 'May be I should drop the idea of arresting her and the man and first of all get my children down to this place.'

I shrugged.

The following day as early as 5 a.m., he took off to the town in his car. He got to the town few minutes after 7 a.m. and went straight to John who was already waiting for him in the office. He quickly took him to the place where he saw the children after a brief exchange of pleasantries.

They waited for a long time at the place before they saw the children going to the school in a man's car. John was the first to see them. He quickly urged Victor to take his car and drive after the car. They drove after the car until it stopped at the entrance of a school.

Victor parked his car behind the man. As the children got out, he called Dotun and her brother. Immediately the children saw their father, they ran wildly to him. They embraced him, crying.

The man that brought them looked puzzled. He got out of the car and went to Victor. 'Who are you?' he asked.

'Let me ask you that question,' Victor said.

'Their mother is my wife,' he said.

'Well,' Victor said, 'I'm the father of these children as you can see from the way they reacted.'

The man looked shocked. 'What do you mean?'

Victor who was getting increasingly angry with him as he said, 'what do I mean? After grabbing my wife, you feel you can grab my children too? Look, if not for a friend of mine that advised me against my decision, I would have brought a policeman to put you and that whore you call your wife into a cooler for kidnapping my children for five months.'

The man looked stunned for a long time. It seemed he was hearing what he had never been told. He looked at Dotun and asked, 'is he really your father?'

Dotun nodded.

'Why didn't you tell me you have a father?'

Victor snorted. 'Who do you think mate with their mother before giving birth to them - wood or stone? Foolish man!'

'Please, forgive me if I sound so foolish,' the man said softly. Victor was really impressed. He looked at John who was silent all the while, looking at the man exchanging words. 'What I was told was different from what I am hearing now. Their mother told me their father was dead and em....'

Victor and John exchanged glances. The man again looked at Dotun and asked again, 'why didn't you tell me you still have a father? You know I love you enough to have taken you back to him if you have told me.'

'My mother warned us not to say anything about him,' Dotun said. 'She said if we say anything about him, she will nearly kill us.'

The man stared at Victor. 'God is my witness. I was convinced she was a widow. That was what she told me. In fact one of the things that made me take her as my wife was because of the emotional condition I thought she was. She... em... said her husband had an accident and his family drove her out of the house and things like that.'

Victor believed was man foolish. How could he put a woman under his roof as a wife without trying to find out her background as the custom demanded? How could he take the children of another person without expecting that at least relation of their father would look for them? Besides, what sort of marriage would he call the type between him and Sarah? Well, Victor concluded at last, he was simply foolish. He hoped he must have learnt to be inquisitive next time.

'Well,' Victor said, ushering his children into his car, 'you can take their mother as your wife. But I cannot allow you to have my children. Good day.'

He got into the car, took John back to the office and went back to his station.

TWO

Things seemed to come back to normal with Victor when he got his children back. He employed a lady to take care of them and to take them to school everyday. On Sundays and at times during the evening on weekdays, he would take the children to the church for services. With his children back in the house, one would have thought Victor was now a happy man. My interaction with him, however, revealed the fact that there was still a vacuum in his life which he tried to fill by playing with the children and going to the church to hear the word of God. Before long, the thought of getting married to another lady began to occur to him. If not for the influence he had gathered through the word of God I normally shared with him and through the sermon in the church, Victor would have probably made proposal to marry the lady that worked in his house. He had once remarked that she was so gentle and obedient, apart from the fact that she was equally as beautiful if not more beautiful than his runaway wife.

'Look,' I told him when he made the remark, 'what you are saying now is a proof that the devil had been talking to you and you have been paying close attention to him. You don't have to tell me you probably wish to marry the lady.'

He looked a little surprised. 'How do you know? I mean what makes you think so.'

'I know when the devil is at work,' I told him. 'Let me share a passage with you in the Bible in the book of Genesis chapter 3 verses 1 to 6.' He gave me a Bible. I opened to the place and began to read. '"Now the serpent was more subtle than any beast of the field which the Lord God had made. And he said unto the woman, Yea, hath God said, ye shall not eat of every tree of the garden?

'"And the woman said unto the serpent, we may eat of the fruit of the trees of the garden:

'"But of the fruit of the tree which is in the midst of the garden, God hath said, ye shall not eat of it, neither shall ye touch it, lest ye die.

'"And the serpent said unto the woman, ye shall not surely die:

'"For God doth know that in the day ye eat thereof, then your eyes shall be opened, and ye shall be as gods, knowing good and evil.

'"And when the woman saw that the tree was good for food, and that, it was pleasant to the eyes, and a tree to be desired to make one wise. She took of the fruit thereof, and did eat, and gave also unto her husband with her; and he did eat."'

I looked up from the Bible at him and said, 'You see, the devil have the same old method to make man rebel against the will of God. See how the devil went to Eve like a soft voiced and intelligent creature, using her eyes and her intelligence to put the entire mankind into problem. The devil appears in many forms. He can appear as a beautiful woman or even as a pastor. You know, of course, that the devil now put on collar to deceive people. Now, I don't want you to misunderstand me. I'm not saying that the lady you employed is a devil's vessel. All I'm saying is that you can get to know the devil working through the things he'll tell you to do. The easiest way of knowing that is to weigh it with the word of God. Even if a pastor comes to tell you anything that contradicts the word, please, spit it out. Don't you ever accept it because God is not going to base his judgment on what the pastor or anybody says but on His word.

'You know you're married to a lady. Though she might have offended you but you have to remember the vow you made to her when you took her to the altar? For better, for worse, you'll be together till death parts you.'

'Not in this case, Pastor Toby,' he said almost harshly. 'You know quite well that God gives us the right to divorce our wives if they commit adultery.'

'Yes, yes, I know,' I said quickly.

'Now tell me,' he continued. 'If you're the one in my position, what would you do? A woman I called my wife went to that extent to ruin my life and you still expect me to take her back?'

'Let me answer your question,' I said. 'If I were in your position, I will still forgive her, at least for God's sake and for the sake of the children.'

He shook his head in disagreement. 'You see, it's easier to counsel a man with such problem than to be in that position.'

'Let me share with you the life of the Spirit filled man I shared in a church. It is in the book of John chapter fourteen. I'll start from verse sixteen. It says: 'And I will pray the Father, and he shall give you another Comforter, that he may abide with you for ever;

'"Even the Spirit of truth; who the world cannot receive, because it seeth him not, neither knoweth him: but you know him; for he dwelleth with you, and shall be with you."'

77

Again I looked at him as he listened attentively. 'You may wonder at what this have got to do with our discussion but you'll soon see the relevance.

'You see, everything in the world has systems. The world has thousand and one reasons why something should not be done and why it cannot be done. But we, Christians have different ways of doing things because we are mandated to do our things in God's way and time. In the book of Isaiah chapter 55 verses 8 and 9 the Bible says: "For my thoughts are not your thoughts, neither are your ways my ways, saith the Lord.

'"For as the heavens are higher than the earth, so are my ways higher than your ways, and my thoughts than your thoughts."

'There is a story in the Bible about a woman that commits adultery. The people brought her case before Jesus and pointed out to him what the law said about adultery. They wanted her stoned to death. The world wants to bring justice to everything that is wrong and in the cause of doing that, they miscarry justice. You see these people who brought the woman failed to recognize the fact that two people were supposed to be involved in adultery. So they brought only one person - the woman. Jesus did not even point out their folly to them. He simply said, "let anybody among you who have not sin throw the first stone." Now they knew that was a point. So they left. They knew that if everybody was to be stoned for the wrong thing he has done, no one would be alive. You see the world have a very foolish way of bringing instant judgment upon a soul. So nobody in this world is qualified to judge any man. That's why Jesus said we must not judge. In essence, I'm not qualified to tell you to put your wife aside because of what she has done. I cannot also say I am qualified to appeal to you to take her back if she decides to come to you. As a matter of fact, I don't think anybody in the world is qualified to judge your case because nobody can claim to be without fault. If everybody is to be judged by the conduct we were once involved in, we'll all be dead. But we have a way of settling things. It is by the word of God. After sharing the word with you, you can then make up your mind what to do about it.

'We are still coming to the issue of the Spirit filled man but I want us to read the passage in Mark chapter 10 verses 4 to 12 which talk about marriage and divorce. It says: "And they said, Moses suffered to write a bill of divorcement, and to put her away.

'"And Jesus answered and said unto them, For the hardness of your heart he wrote you this precept.

'"But from the beginning of the creation God made them male and

78

female.

'"For this cause shall a man leave his father and mother, and cleave to his wife;

'"And they twain shall be one flesh: so then they are no more twain but one flesh.

'"What therefore God bath joined together, let not man put asunder.

'"And in the house his disciples ask him again of the matter.

'"And he saith unto them, whosoever shall put away his wife, and marry another committeth adultery against her.

'"And if a woman shall put away her husband, and be married to another, she committeth adultery."' I looked at him when I finished reading.

'There is a funny story in the book of Hosea chapter one,' I said after a pause. 'God told the man of God to marry a prostitute. He married her and she gave birth to three children. Now when you look at that, you begin to think the man was crazy but then God has a purpose for doing a thing. I'm sure people who knew the man of God and the prostitute will say, "that guy must be crazy. They must have cursed him from their house." But the thought of the man of God was different from their thoughts because his thought was the thought of God which is different from man's.

'Now let's continue on the talk of the Spirit filled man. He is comforted by the Holy Spirit even in the stormy situation - even in the ocean of insanity. Remember, in the ocean of insanity' that is making everybody to become insane, if the Spirit filled man keeps his sanity in Christ, he will survive in the ocean. Apart from this, the man will know the truth. The word of God is the truth and God Himself is the truth. Why do you think people are following the trend of the world? It is because they don't have the truth. If they know the truth, they will not swindle. If they know the truth, they will not defraud public fund nor tell lies. If we are all to be put behind the bars for all the wrong things we have done in the secret, we'll all be in jail. But Jesus set us free and said, 'take up your cross and follow me.' Cross is a sign of suffering and endurance.

'Your wife does not know the truth. That's probably the reason she treated you like this. But I want you too to think of the person you have offended. If they were to bounce on you too, what do you think will happen?'

After saying so much, he asked me, 'you mean I should take back that whore if she comes back.'

'I never say you should and I never say you shouldn't,' I replied.

'From what you're saying,' he said, 'you want me to take her if she comes back.'

'Well,' I shrugged.

'You know,' he said, 'I can only forgive her but I can never take her back. The reason is that a woman like that is dangerous to be kept in the house. She can even poison me.'

I smiled as I said, 'I am convinced that you're a believer. As a believer, has it ever occurred to you that some supernatural forces back everything that happens in this world?'

'How do you mean?' he asked.

'Let me explain by sharing with you what happened to a woman who is one of our church members. This woman suddenly began to have problem with her husband after spending about seven years living together with their two children. The man was not yet born-again then but he was naturally kind to people. He so much cared for his family that he was ready to wait on any of them. You know what I mean. But then, no matter how good or nice a person is, the devil can still mess up his life if he is not born again. Guess what happened. One of the neighbours who was very jealous of the family planted a juju charm in the house that turns the man into a violent person. All of a sudden; things began to go wrong in the family. The man who was once known a loving husband became a terror overnight. The woman went through a terrible ordeal. The problem in that house became so much that I had to come in. You wouldn't believe this. The man threatened to break my head if I didn't leave the house. Right n my presence, the man wanted to beat the woman senseless if I had not intervened. Later, the woman told me that's how he used to beat her. This woman had been rushed to the hospital for treatments several times while fighting with her. In fact, it got to the point that I was forced to advise the woman to leave the man for a while. Guess what. The woman insisted on staying with him. She said that if God would not prevail on him, she was prepared to die. We were all challenged in the church to pray with her. One day, while having a revival service in the church, we suddenly saw the man. God must have led him into the church. He was touched by the message, especially when the guest speaker told him that the problem in his family was caused by the juju charm planted in his house. They got home and searched the house thoroughly. They found the charm in their bedroom. No one could explain how it got there. There was peace in the house after the charm was removed.

80

'I must tell you that it was his wife's perseverance that brought deliverance into the house. When I was bordered that she may be hurt if she stayed with the man, she said she was ready to die if God did not intervene. Since God cannot bear to loose any of His children that way, the woman gave Him no other option but to intervene. It is not the act of a person that should be addressed in this case but the spirit behind it. In other words, if she had married another man, who can tell whether she would have been dead by now or whether she would have lost her salvation? You see, at times, some things happening in people's lives could be connected with spiritual things. Your wife as a matter of fact, is under the influence of bad spirit. If this bad spirit is replaced with the Spirit of God in her life, you'll see the perfect image of God in her.'

About two weeks after that, as if God wanted me to have that discussion with him before his wife came back, I suddenly saw her in my house while my family and me took our lunch.

'Come and take some food,' my wife told her after exchanging pleasantries with her.

She shook her head slowly and sadly. I already knew what had brought her.

'Have you gone home?' I asked her, looking at the bag she was holding.

She nodded. She looked as if she would burst out crying any moment. I left my food and took her to the veranda to have a talk with her.

She didn't know I know all that had happened until I said, 'why did you do that?'

She began to tell me a story that was different from what Victor told me although there were some similarities. 'Actually, sir,' she said tearfully, 'I didn't know what went wrong with me. I was happy with him before one of my friends told me he used to keep some ladies whenever I went out. I was made to believe many untrue things about him. Someone advised me to go to a church where some prophecies came out about my husband and me. I was told he was planning to poison my food and that I should take my time with him. It was there I met a man who I later elope with.'

'Did you try to sell his house?' I asked.

'Yes, actually,' she replied. 'I wanted to ruin him before he ruined me as I was made to believe.'

'The man you elope with,' I said, 'knows your husband is still alive?'

She hesitated for a while before she said, 'actually, I... em... he knows but the church told me to marry him.'

I studied her face for sometimes. Of course, I knew she was not telling the whole truth. 'Why not tell me what actually happened. God can only have mercy on you if you confess your sin to him.'

'I'm telling the truth, sir,' she said.

'I happened to know some things, which you don't think I know. The only way you can get God on your side is to say the truth - the whole truth and nothing but the truth. If you tell me all you did, I won't condemn you. I'm sure God will not condemn you but if you hide the truth, that means you have not yet repented. Forgiveness cannot come without repentance.'

She hesitated for along time before she said, 'I'm guilty. I'm the cause of the whole problem.'

'That's not what I want to hear,' I said, getting a little annoyed. 'I want you to tell me exactly what happened.'

'My friends actually told me my husband was having an affair. So I decided to take my revenge on him by moving out with men. Then I ...em... I'm ashamed but the false church I got involved with fuel the problem in my home. I was told to burn candles and do some things that look like rituals. I was told my husband wanted to kill me. So I must do something about it. I was introduced to a man who just lost his wife. I was told to lie to the man that I too just lost my husband.'

I was shaking my head sorrowfully. I knew the world is full of evil but I never knew that the devil could go as far as putting his messengers to pose as messengers of God. Well, I thought, we are really at the end time when a lot of evil things are happening.

When she finished telling her version of the story up to the time she was forced to come back, I told her of the need to give her life to Christ. She actually came back because the man she was leaving with could not put up with her any longer coupled with the fact that she could not stand being away from her children.

'You need to be born again, my sister.'

'But I used to go to church,' she said.

'Going to church is not being born-again,' I said. 'You may be going to church for many years and still remain a sinner, especially if you're going to the church where truth is not preached or where truth is distorted. You see, being born-again is a personal experience. It's between you and God.'

'How do I become born-again then?' she asked slowly and thoughtfully.

'You simply have to accept Jesus Christ as your Lord and Saviour. You confess your sin to him and renounce it.'

That moment she decided to give her life to Christ but I knew time would tell if she merely did that so that I could resolve the conflict between her and her husband.

While going to Victor's house, she told me that as soon as Victor set eyes on her, he drove her out as if she was a leper.

Victor was in the room when we got to his house. I knocked at the door. He angrily asked, 'who is it?'

'It's Pastor,' I said. I told his wife to find a place to stay while I talked with him.

After he had allowed me in, I went to sit down with him in the sitting room. From the expression on his face, I could see that he knew what had brought me. 'Remember the discussion we were having together the other time?'

He nodded reluctantly.

'I want us to conclude it today,' I said.

'I really don't have much time, Pastor Toby, please,' he said.

'This could be the only chance we have to talk about God,' I said.

He looked at my face for a long time. 'Why are you trying to play on my intelligence.' he said. 'She was here. So...'

'I knew she was here,' I said. 'But we never know she'll be coming before we had the first discussion about her, do we?'

'So what?'

'So God could have probably been directing our discussion then.'

'Okay,' he said. 'What have you got to say now?'

'Both of us need a Bible.'

Without saying anything, he went to get two Bibles. He gave me one and took the other one.

'Let's open to the book of I Corinthians chapter 7 verse 12 which says, "But to the rest speak I, not the Lord: If any brother hath a wife that believe not, and she be pleased to dwell with him, let him not put her away." Again see what verse 16 of the same chapter says, "For what knowest thou, O wife, whether thou shalt save thy husband? Or knowest thou, O man. whether thou shalt save thy wife"'

Victor scratched his chin thoughtfully. 'But that's talking to those who don't believe alone, not an adulterer.'

'What do you expect from someone who doesn't believe?' I asked. 'They are the same. It is unbelief in the word of God that makes someone an unbeliever. It is unbelief that makes a person an adulterer or fornicator. As a matter of fact, the worst sin in a man is

83

unbelief. If someone believes the word of God, he will not sin again.'

Victor looked rather confused.

'This may be too hard for you,' I said. 'But that is the truth. You know within you that you can tolerate her but you just want to force her out of your life.'

'Why do you think so?'

'You once tolerated her before the incidence became aggravated,' I said. 'Besides, you have been husband and wife for many years before all these started. As I can see the case, even the marriage act that was established to see to matrimonial problem will not permit you to divorce her.' I smiled when I saw his puzzled expression. 'The reason is that you have no ground to do away with your wife.'

'Even on the ground of adultery?' he asked, looking confused the more.

'Adultery alone is not a ground for divorce,' I replied. 'It must be with the proof that you cannot tolerate it.' I paused to smile at him again. 'Ask any good lawyer, he'll tell you this.'

There was a brief thoughtful silence.

'If the law made by man will go to any extent to discourage divorce, how much more God who instituted the marriage?'

He was beginning to look sober.

'Brother Victor,' I continued in a gentle voice. 'God hates divorce. That is why Jesus who happens to be our spiritual husband never turns us - miserable sinners away. He loves us and died for our sins even though we don't deserve his love. He died for you and me so that we won't die the second time in hell. Both of us me know all we have done to him but he never rejects us when we asked him to forgive us. Why then must you reject your wife who came to you for forgiveness?'

Something quite unexpected came out from his mouth. He said in a very quiet voice. 'I'm sorry.'

That was all I needed to hear before I went to call his wife outside.

As soon as she entered, she went on kneels tearfully.

Victor looked thoughtful.

'Well,' I said, 'your wife wants to know if you have forgiven her.'

He stood up after a moment, pulled her up on her feet and embraced her.

I took my leave immediately because I knew the problem was over.

Happiness began in the family after the re-union.

THREE GENERATIONS AGO

ONE

Kunle lies comfortably on the bed with his hand supporting his head, trying to conjure the events that took place three generations ago. His great grandmother called Madam Peter who died long before he was born told his grandmother the story about herself with the desire to teach every member of the family, especially the young adults not to yield to the lust of the flesh.

With his remarkable sense of imagination, he pictured all the scenes in the story as if he was there when the whole events took place, putting many loose ends together to make the story clear and coherent. Even though, as he was told, life then was quite different from the modern life back then, he fixed all the missing links perfectly, making the story acceptable to a modern person without offending his sense of imagination.

His great grandmother was called Mojisola when she was a maiden. The interpretation of the name in Yoruba ethnic group in Nigeria is "coming into fortune". It was an irony if not ridiculous to think of someone from a wretched background with such a bogus name. In these modern days Mojisola would have fallen into the class of the under privileged. So her name was apparently too bogus to reveal her true background. Perhaps, her father who was a poor peasant had the intention to dignify her among his other children by giving her such name.

Lere, Mojisola's father was not only just poor but very rustic and naïve. He seemed contented with his daily pay which was next to nothing. He didn't seem to have any idea how to improve the condition of his family. He made his wife and children rely so much on his daily pay that none of them would eat without it. Consequently, whenever there was no pay, there would be no food. They lived from hand to mouth and on many occasions, there was nothing in the hand to put into their mouths. Like every other children in the family, Mojisola was not well fed although her charm as outstanding. She was born like every other poor child in the village, without any silver spoon in her mouth.

Her mother became pregnant of her while trying to perform her duty as a wife to her father. For the nine months she carried her, she ate herbs and vegetables because the family could not afford the exorbitant charge of the native doctors. In those days, there was no medical treatment. The doctors then were herbalists, most of whom caused brain damages while trying to cure headaches. Even then, only the rich could afford going to the herbalists for their services were too expensive. Also among these herbalists were another set those who always demanded for the fattest goat or chicken in the market to procure a cure for ailments from the gods. Of course, the sacrifice of such animals were always done with their cooking pots with the gods who dwelled in their belly saying," peace be unto you." The gods might be kind enough to give part of the animals to the patients. In most cases, the patients worsened or died of the ailments which simple herbs could have cured. If the patients survived, they thanked the gods that cured them. If they died, no one questioned the gods because they gave lives and they could as well take them.

Mojisola's mother took the risk to give birth to her without the help of the so called gods or their agents. She felt Mojisola probing to get out of her womb with her head. She simply went into her room to allow Mojisola to come in to the world. Her father ran into the room when he heard her cries. The mother wrapped her in a tick cloth after she had removed every traces of the delivery and presented the precious gift to him. Mojisola was born and bred in the family where hunger reigned. The condition was at the dying state. Not really dying as such but rather counting the number of days which they have survived the blood and thunder of administrations of poverty and hunger

Lere found an unusual employer among many others whom he had worked for. He was employed for four days in the man's farm. Apart from the efforts Lere had put in the job, his family had starved for those days. They have only managed to get themselves one meal each day. They all anticipated that by the end of the four days, Lere would have gotten his pay and the family could live in luxuries for few days by eating enough food everyday.

But then, Lere's employer was someone who took every opportunity he has to make money out of other people's sweat. He saw Lere as an ideal man to make money from. So out of sheer greed, he delayed paying him the wage.

'Sir, 'Lere said, 'how could you do a thing like that? I worked hard on your farm for days and you refused to pay me.'

'I didn't say I'll not pay the money, did I?' Lere's employer said, 'I say I'll pay you next week when things are fine with me.'

87

'How do I feed my family?' Lere asked involuntarily.

'You can always find a way to feed them.'

'All right 'Lere said. 'I think I know how to feed them.' He went home to meet his family who were anxiously waiting for him to bring home the family fortune - food. Lere didn't look worried at all. He said, 'well, I haven't got the money. It will be ready next week. You don't have to border what we'll eat till then. We'll all go to my employer and live with him until he is able to pay us our money.'

Good idea, every member of the family seemed to be saying. It was about time they had a taste of what rich people eat. They all put on their best cloths which were not even as good as what an average person wore in the street. They robbed their faces that were battered with hardship with the last drops of palm oil in the house and got ready to pay Lere's employer the most spectacular visit he had ever had.

The family got to the house. Lere was the first to enter the house. His employer was sitting comfortably on the wooden chair with pounded yam with mouth watering vegetable soup and assorted meat, drinking from a big calabash of fresh palm wine. Lere did not look offended or disappointed to see the man who claimed he had no money to pay him eating and drinking items that were worth more than what he owned him.

The employer looked startled to see him. He soon jumped on his feet when hungry looking visitors poured into his cosy sitting room.

Lere gestured each member of his family to take a seat each. 'Well, sir,' he said, ' 'm sorry to disturb your peace. As you can see we are not as comfortable without food. We've come to stay with you until all my money is paid. We've not come here so that you'll pay me immediately-no, far from it. We've only come here as a visitor. We'll eat whatever you eat and we'll drink whatever you drink

Was the employer startled? May be he was not .But the visit was not too funny. It was a serious case, especially when a family man felt no qualms about bringing his wife and children to be fed all because he owned him some chicken feed.

'Now wait a minute,' the employer said, looking round at Lere's family members that looked so hungry that they were ready to eat anything that tested like food. With the hungry bunch in his house, he didn't feel secured They could bounce on him and order him to give them food or even tear him apart like hungry lions.

'You don't have to worry, 'Lere said. 'There's no problem. We've come here as visitors. So you can give us whatever you have in your house.

'Give me a second, would you?' the employer said. That minute he went to get all Lere's money. Nobody could tell where he got it from. He counted the money to him and muttered under breath, 'take your money and pack your loads trouble out of my house!'

He never engaged Lere again .To him, he had more than enough trouble he could cope with. There was no way he could possibly make money out of someone with so many parasites.

Lere managed to get a piece of land from his extended family but he needed a lot of money to cultivate it. So he applied for a loan from a man who is a modern person would have called Vulture. Vulture was very rich but he was the type of man people of modern days would have eliminated, not only because he charged exorbitant interest on the loan but else demanded for an "Iwofa" because he can not imagine it, especially when slavery had long ago gone out of history. Slavery had become extinct but she left a baby behind called Iwofa. The practice of Iwofa was barbarian if not devastating to humanity .Iwofa didn't exactly look like her mammy. She looked quite reasonable but the similarity between her and slavery was remarkable. They were both total loss of freedom and a nightmare.

In the ancient times in Yoruba ethnic group, a man who wished to borrow money from another person must provide an Iwofa who would serve as collateral for the loan. In the modern day, properties are used as collateral but in this case only human beings , preferably , the child of the borrower was always required the person that was used as a collateral would live with the lender until the load and the interest were paid in full. Of course, the Iwofa would work as a slave till the time he or she was redeemed.

Vulture asked for Mojisola as an Iwofa, not only because she was very beautiful and cool headed but also because he could take her as his bed mate when she grew up if her father could not pay the loan as he thought. He anticipated that Lere would not be able to pay the amount he was asking for because by the time he might be ready to pay, the interest he charged on the loan would have accumulated. Of course, Lere could not envisage this because he was so ignorant.

Out of sheer ignorance, Lere gave Mojisola to Vulture as collateral for the loan. Vulture capitalized on his ignorance and quickly entered into an agreement with him according to the agreement, Lere would not have Mojisola back nor be given in marriage to anyone until the loan and all the interest have been paid.

Lere sincerely believed that he would be able to redeem her daughter when he might have gathered the harvest on the farm. But

89

then, the harvest for that year was a disaster as there was no much rainfall. Apart from the interest which had accumulated, lere was unable to pay anything out of the loan as the first instalment, making the debt to be to huge for him to settle. The little harvest he was able to gather on the farm was wholly consumed by his family.

Lere and his family watched Mojisola helplessly becoming a full time slave. It was apparent to everybody that Mojisola was beyond redemption. The feelings of guilt that he had sold his precious daughter to vulture made lere turned into an alcoholic. He took cheap locally made gin. He was constantly drunk because each time he was sober, the thought of Mojisola as a slave always broke his heart. In time being, he because a very irresponsible husband and father. He spent every kobo he made to buy gin, the rest of his family were compelled to take up the challenge of life by becoming cheap labourers.

Within a short period lere died. It was a painful loss to the family, especially when they knew what attributed to his untimely death.

Vulture allowed Mojisola to attend her father's burial. The rest of the family were delighted to see her though, they knew that she was no longer a member of the family. She was as a matter of fact a bond girl that has no hope of either getting married or getting her freedom.

The local priest who conducted the funeral services talked extensively about Jesus to everybody that was present at the cemetery he read from the bible in Luke chapter 15 verses 7 to 10 " I say unto you, that likewise joy shall be in heaven over sinner that repentedth, more than over ninety nine just persons which need no repentance. " Either what woman having ten pieces of silver, if she lose one piece, doth not light a candle, and sweep the house, answer seek diligently till she find it?

'And when she hath found it, she calleth her friends and her neighbours together, saying, rejoice with me, for I have found the piece which I had lost.

'Likewise, I say unto you, there is joy in the presence of the angels of God over one sinner that repenteth." The priest paused to look at the audience. 'We all have to bury the dead but it will be very essential to tell you that we shall all die one day. Therefore we must be concerned with eternity…. I cannot say anything about the dead now because I am not to be so concerned about him but rather to be concerned about those alive. I want to tell you that unless you repent of your sin, there is no hope for you in heaven. This world is not a place for joy but rather a place that will determine your eternity….

90

The sermon of the priest was so touching that big drops of tears rolled down Mojisola's cheeks.

The priest, just like every other people thought she was crying over her dead father until he went to her to console her.

'It's okay, 'the priest said. 'Well, what can I do for you now?

'I want you to give me a bible,' she said.

The priest looked a little surprised. 'Bible? Do you know how to read?'

She shook her head sadly. 'But I think if Jesus whom you told me about is real, he would teach me whom you told me about is real, he would teach me how to read or send someone to teach me.'

The priest quickly gave her his bible. Of course, bibles at that time were so scarce but he could not turn down Mojisola's request.

In spite of the bondage Mojisola found herself, she began to experience certain peace and joy which she could not understand. She worked as a slave for long hours yet she still found time to talk to God in the way she understood. She looked inside the bible even though she could not read if. She could imagine Jesus speaking to her through those words which she could not read yet the meaning was transmitted into her heart. On many occasion, she would whisper, 'Lord Jesus, I cherish you. I wish I can read your words.'

TWO

As weeks rolled into months, Mojisola began to get familiar with some words. They looked like beautiful drawings. They were "Lord God", "Thus says" "be courageous" "be strong", and many others like that. She managed to draw all the words in a sheet of paper the way she saw them in the bible and began to look for some one to explain the words. As there were few people that could read in the village, it took her time to find someone who managed to interpret what they meant to her. She felt God was telling her to be courageous and strong. The man that interpreted the words to her suddenly developed interest in reading the bible with her. She soon learned from the man how to read and write even in the mix of hardship.

Mojisola began to grow into a young beautiful lady despite the bondage. As she grew, her belief in Christ became stronger with constant reading of the bible. She was able to grow in wisdom and understanding of God's way. Although she was not too happy about her life, she hoped that when she died, she would meet her Lord.

Vulture observed that Mojisola was not the little Iwofa she had taken from Lere but a very beautiful lady with outstanding virtues. In fact, he was forced to admit that she was different from all that ladies he had known since his fifty sixty year old life. He began to find ways to make her his wife.

One day, he invited her to dine with him. Mojisola who had never received such invitations from him quickly guessed that something strange was about to happen. With prayerful mind, she accepted the invitation.

She sat in front of him, uncertain of how to behave in his presence after taken some food out of the plate, vulture said herself to vulture to be used to fulfil his lustful desire for just one year and then pray for forgiveness of sin from did that, no one could redeem her. No sane person who probably wanted to marry her would pay such huge money for her sake. So she didn't have option but to consider vulture's offer.

She prayed about it, saying, Lord, you know I want to do your will to be free and get married so that I can serve you better.

Then she felt the urge to read the book of John chapter 8 verses 32 to 37 within her spirit. She got the bible answer began to read, 'And ye shall know the truth, and the truth shall make you free.

"They answered him, we be Abraham's seed, and were never in bondage to any man: how sayest thou, ye shall know the truth, and the truth shall make you free.

"Jesus answered them, verily, verily, I say unto you, whosoever committeth sin is the servant of sin.

"And the servant abideth not in the house for ever: but the son abideth ever.

"If the son therefore shall make you free, ye shall be free indeed.

"I know that ye are Abraham's seed; but ye seek to kill me, because my word hath no place in you."

When she finished reading, she began to meditate on the passage. God seemed to be telling her that she was not in bondage as she thought because once Jesus had set her free from the bondage of sin, she was free indeed. She was no longer a slave as far as God was concerned but a child of God. If she sinned by taking vulture's offer, she would be a real slave to him and to sin. More so, if she was really the child of God, she would not think of nailing Jesus the second time on the cross by offering her body to vulture.

Suddenly she began to cry. By that passage, she knew she had to choose between Jesus and vulture who promised to give her freedom. 'Lord,' she said, 'I'll rather be an Iwofa and be your child than to be a slave to sin by giving myself to my master.'

Almost everyday, she was faced with the temptation to accept 'Mojisola, you know you're a pretty lady now.

"Thank you, sir,' he went on, 'you'll be thinking of how to get married. Aren't you thinking of that?'

'Well, sir,' Mojisola said, feeling some excitement within her, 'you never encouraged me about it.'

'Oh, really,' Vulture said, 'you never bordered me about it.'

'You want to set me free, sir?' Mojisola asked involuntarily.

'Well em, yes,' Vulture said. 'I want to set you free so that you can become my wife.'

Mojisola looked rather surprised. She was just eighteen year old girl and she could not imagine herself marrying a man that was old enough to be her grand father.

'Oh, no, sir,' Mojisola said. 'I cannot marry you, sir. The reason is that you've got a wife already who could be regarded as my mother.

93

Vulture looked annoyed. He stood up suddenly and ordered her out of his presence. 'Well, we'll see who will lose. If the loan your father took from me is not paid with the interest, you'll be an Iwofa for the rest of your life.'

Mojisola became sorrowful. She could have taken the step a modern person would have taken. She could run away or poison vulture in order to get her freedom but she couldn't because she feared God.

When Vulture saw that he could not succeed with the first plan, he came up with another one. He invited her again to dine with her and then asked if she could get her freedom. His intension was to make her pregnant and then use that means to make her his wife.

It was a big temptation to her, especially when she was of marriageable age. But then, there was God to consider would she be justified to defile her body all because she was looking for freedom? From the look of things, there was no way she could be redeemed unless she did what vulture requested. She could give offer which vulture persistently gave to her but she maintained her stand. She rejected it each day he made it. Of course, this made him very hostile. He made her worked harder than ever and gave her little rest.

One day, Mojisola sat under a free after she had worked for several hours; thinking of her life. She thought of her family who vulture had denied her from meeting. She thought of her blink future. She thought of other ladies who had hopes of getting married. She thought of her father and her brothers and sisters and her poor mother who was getting weary of life. Then before she knew it, drops of tears began to roll down from her eyes.

There was a British missionary driving a bicycle along that sick at that time. He was coming from another village to hold a crusade for the people in that village.

He stopped from a distance when he saw Mojisola. Feeling great compassion for her, he went to her and asked her, 'what's wrong, young lady?'

Mojisola looked at him and knelt down in front of him. 'I am a very sorrowful person,' she said, 'because I'm an Iwofa. My master offered to set me free if only I can be his bed mate for one year. I happen to be a Christian. So I cannot do that, he made life so miserable for me. It . . seemed .... God is so far from me and .... I'm trying to reach him.'

The missionary was moved the more. Tears rolled down from his own eyes too. He said, 'you shall be free, young lady. You shall be redeemed by the lord Jesus. Now take me to your master.'

94

It was like a dream as the missionary demanded the agreement between him and Mojisola's father when he met with vulture.

At first, vulture roared with laughter when the missionary told him he wanted to redeem Mojisola. He calculated the amount needed to redeem her and laughed even more loudly.

The missionary went away and came back few days later after getting donations from co missionaries in the country and his friends in other places.

Vulture was stunned when he brought the money and demanded to go with Mojisola

Mojisola gained back her freedom that day. Even then, it was like a dream.

She began to work with the missionary and later got married to his nephew who was a pastor.

Kunle sighed when he returned from the journey of three generations ago and said to himself, 'my great grand mother was really Mojisola. Finding Christ alone was enough for her to come into great fortune.'

CHECK OUT OTHER BOOKS BY DIPO TOBY ALAKIJA
Each Serves Either As Edifying Or Evangelical Or Missionary Or Academic Tool At Home, School, Bible Clubs, Sunday Schools, Church, Office And Other Fellowships

NO MORE TEARS TO SHED
ISBN: 978-49874-3-0 ISBN: 978-978-74-3-1

Kidnappers took Tokunbo away from his grand parents in a city in Nigeria when he was a little boy. A nice woman found him in another town and gave him a false identity. She spoilt him with love, making him to grow into a rebellious teenager that was not appreciated anywhere. When Janet made him a Christian, however, life began to make sense to him until the day he was beaten to the point of death for the offence he knew nothing about. He left the town for the city which, unknown to him, held his true identity and the link to his parents in the United States. To find them was only a question of time.

FOOTSTEPS IN THE MUD
ISBN: 978-36348-9-5 ISBN: 978-978-36348-9-3
The Drama Package Of Results Of Research Works That trace Global And Societal Vices To The Corrupt Or Lost Of Family Values

The 13-Episode drama book involves Bosede who learnt many wrong things from her parents' conduct and foul language. She was forced to marry Kola when she became pregnant. Using her mother's method to handle her father, she tried to subject Kola to her control. In the course of that, she made life terrible for him. Although her mother tried to warn her of the implications of maltreating her husband but Bosede has grown out of control. Consequently, while looking for peace, Kola was pushed out of the house. He made friends with some guys who taught him the unholy ways of life and influenced him to become a menace in the house.

Junior who was born at time the couple never proved to be responsible parents also learnt wrong things from them. He decided to follow his father's footsteps by taking alcohol when he was in primary school. As if that was not bad enough, he tried to teach other children in the school the madness in his home. A school teacher, however, was able to influence him and his mother by teaching them Christian morals. Even then, Junior was soon caught in the crossfire at home as his father tried to enlist him as a future member of a secret cult that posed as a social club.

SUCCESSFUL CHRISTIANITY AND BASIC MINISTRIES
ISBN: 978-49874-6-0
A Collection Of Resource Materials That Precedes Christian Ministries And Basic Leadership Course Book

The first question is how Christianity is practiced even in a hostile environment. Next to that is the question about the potentials of Christians in spite of their apparent limitations. The other issues are connected to the successes, deliverance, callings, basic ministries of all Christians and evangelism.  Various schools of thoughts have attempted these questions but many answers only portray Christianity as a form of religion instead of a way of life as specified by God. Some answers give room for compromise, hypocrisies, dogmas and denominational doctrines. The misconceptions about these areas of Christianity have brought about worldliness instead of righteousness and false achievements instead of fulfillment.

This book which contains six different subjects had been used to hold seminars at various levels, train ministers and Christian workers in Bible Schools and to equip the Church. It explains in simple terms the seemingly complex issues on practice of Christianity, Potentials, Deliverance, God's Kind Of Success, Evangelism and Basic Ministries of a Christian with Biblical principles, life transforming stories and illustrations.

CHRISTIAN MINISTRIES AND BASIC LEADERSHIP
ISBN: 978-36348-7-9 ISBN: 978-978-36348-7-9
A Collection Of Resource Materials That Follows Up Successful Christianity And Basic Ministries Course Book

As it is common to say that the hood does not make a monk, the dignified positions and bogus titles of many Christian leaders in modern days do not really make them Gospel Ministers.

This course book - a compilation of five resource materials on Missions And Outreach Ministries, Christian Communication Arts, Christian Leadership, Christian Education Methodology and Ministries Of Improvisations - aims at making every matured Christian an effective minister and leader at their respective homes, communities and nations. It teaches various ways Christians can communicate the word of God, meeting up to their responsibilities as ministers and leaders that reconcile people to God, edifying the Body Of Christ and reaching out to souls at the same time.

All of the resource materials are in use in Bible Schools like College

Of Christian Education And Missions, in Churches and other ministries to raise Christian workers, Evangelists, Missionaries and other Ministers that serve at various levels and leadership capacities.

INSANITY OF HUMANITY

ISBN: 978-36348-6-0 ISBN: 978-978-36348-6-2

The Results Of Research Works Into Various Methods Of Brainwashing

Man is made to exercise his freewill. The mind of his own and the power to choose between right and wrong, good and evil, light and darkness is about to be washed away through brainwashing. The agents of control dubbed as Secret Government by John Todd (the top Illuninati defector) have put necessary machinery in place to ensure that all human beings are in conformity in their thinking and ways of life, trying to wipe away diversity, which makes each person unique.

This book attempts to shed light on how the techniques of mind control are applied through the use of propaganda, education, entertainments, drugs, religions, media and other means of communications. It is the result of research works, some of which are based on findings of various researchers and writers like Bugger Lugz, Edward Hunter, Hadley Cantril, Herbert Krugman, David L. Robb, Vaughan Bell, Juliana Gomez, Ryan Duffy Vice, Henry Makow, David Nicholls, Fritz Springmeire, Steven Hassan, Renate Thienel, Debra Pursell, Mary Pride and a host of others who are acknowledged in this book.

THE BATTLE OF THE CONQUERORS

ISBN: 978-49874-7-3 ISBN: ISBN: 978-978-49874-0-7-9

Wickedness takes over the land of Bondage from First Couple and subjects everybody into slavery without giving anybody the chance to be free. Love brings The Redeemer from Eternity and offers the slaves the chance to escape. Wickedness soon declares war and engages everyone in the battle. The Redeemer makes the redeemed people Conquerors by giving them the armour of war and Comforter but Wickedness cannot be undone. He has several thousands of years of experience in the war. So he is quick to recognize the weakness of the redeemed people who are ignorant of their strengths and advantages. Although the Conquerors fight like immutable giants, rescuing victims of war, many people suffer heavy casualties.

Since King Wickedness knows that a redeemed person is strong enough to chase one thousand of his warriors at a time, and two would put ten thousand into flight, he enlists as one of his warriors the people's deadliest enemy called Disunity.

Wickedness is able to strike the people by making them to fight with one another, turning what is supposed to be their best moments in the battle into tales of woes.

BLOODSHED IN CAMPUS
ISBN: 978-07350-3-8 ISBN: 978-978-7350-3-6

A poor widow tearfully warned her son, Richard, against joining the bad wagon when he got an admission into one of the Nigerian Universities. He resisted the membership of groups of students, including the Christian Fellowship until he had an encounter with a member of The Black Skulls - a deadly and ruthless secret cult on the campus.

Before Richard knew what he was up against, the head of The Black Skulls had arranged items for his initiation into the cult. While resisting being initiated, he ran to the Christian Fellowship for help. The leader of the Christian Fellowship dragged The President of Students' Union Government (S.U.G) into the conflict. With the involvement of the S.U.G President, another formidable cult called The Red Eyes felt obliged to team up against The Black Skulls. Then the campus turned into a battlefield and BLOODSHED became the order of the black day.

NETWORK BIBLE CLUB
YOUTH AND ADULT BOOK ONE
ISBN: 978 - 978- 49874-9-X ISBN: 978-978-49874-9-3
A collection of 26 life transforming stories, 26 poems, 26 hymn tuned songs and weekly Bible lessons

The issue of moral instructions in schools and at homes is threatened with extinction. Consequently, so many youths are involved in prostitution, drug addictions, cultism, fraudulent practices, armed robberies and other crimes. Those who are supposed to be trained as leaders in various walks of life are the ones posing serious threats to many lives. Many parents who fail to add moral values to the upbringing of their children often times breed potential criminals under their roofs without knowing it. Apart from these, many other people negatively influence young ones through the media, music, publications, films, conduct and foul language; making them to lose their moral and family values.

This book one just like the rest of other volumes is an attempt to bring back moral instructions into schools and campuses through the use of stories, hymn tuned songs, poems, Bible lessons and class activities. It is designed to assist teachers and ministers in Secondary Schools, Bible Clubs, Churches and Campus Fellowships to teach people, especially youths the Word of God and serves as a school text book in subjects relating to literature, music and other creative works.

FOUNDATION BIBLE CLUB A-Z STORY BOOK
ISBN: 978-49874-2-2 ISBN: 978-978-49874-2-4
Volume 1 With 26 Stories, 26 Bible
Lessons, 26 Rhymes And 26 Songs For Book For Young Minds

An adage says, "a man who builds a house without building his child builds what the child will later sell." Proverbs 22:6 says, "train up a child in the way he should go: and when he is old, he will not depart from it." This book is an attempt to assist parents and teachers to meet up to the challenges that befall them in carrying out this important function in the light of the moral decadence that is prevailing all over the world.

The first edition of the book was used by several thousands of teachers, ministers and parents in schools, Churches and homes to build the moral values of young ones. Apart from the stories, songs and Bible passages for the young ones to study, there is a seminar material that is based on the lecture which the author delivered to school proprietors, children ministers and Christian professionals in this volume.

RANSOM FOR LOVE
ISBN: 978-49874-8-1 ISBN: 978-978-4987-4-8-6

She accepted his marriage proposal without knowing the kind of person he was. She soon discovered that he was a mean and ruthless guy who was always ready to get whatever he wanted by all means even if he has to pay for it with the lives of others. She was in his bondage, especially when her parents who believed he was a generous and gentleman were on his side.

Because she considered the proposal to marry him as a marriage engagement with the devil incarnate, she decided that she would rather die than to share her life with him. Then out of the blues, this passionate gentleman sneaked into her life despite all she did to discourage him. She could not resist his love for her when he offered to set her free from the devil incarnate. Then the battle began – sooner than they anticipated.

THE WEIGHT OF DEATH

ISBN: 9978-36348-0-1 ISBN: 978-978-36348-0-0

(Story Of The Spirit Eyes Series)

PLAY ONE: HORROR IN THE FAMILY: Talimi probably did not envisage his death when he was trying to compel his son, Damola to succeed him in the occult Brotherhood. Other members of the secret cult were aware of the battle between them. So when Talimi died; his family, especially Damola who was a diehard Christian began to fall prey to the cult. Using all their powers and the spirit that posed as Talimi's ghost, the cult waged war against the family, tormenting and making them to be at loggerheads.

PLAY TWO: RITUAL KIDS' KIDNAPPERS: Victor and the rest of the members of the School Bible Club were taught that there are lots of evil people in this world but he did not understand why God allowed him to be among the children that were taken away from their parents. He soon understood that he was to be used by God to rescue other children who did not know that everyone that truly believes in Jesus has the power to overcome evil.

PLAY THREE: THE WEIGHT OF DEATH: Awoseun would not have known the real source of problems of mankind if his father had not given him the power to see demons tormenting the people in different ways. What he was yet to know, however, was the power of light over darkness. When he was caught in crossfire between these powers, he desperately sought for deliverance.

CALVARY ROCK RESOURCE BOOKLETS
ISSN: 1595 93X

The Quarterly Missionary Booklets That Are Designed To Teach Children, Youths And Adults In Schools, Fellowships, Churches, At Homes, Office And Other Places.

Although all the various volumes of this booklet can be used independently of other books but it is recommended that it should be used as part of supplementary materials to make up for Foundation and Network Bible Club Story Books for both children and adults in School, Church, Campus, Office and other Fellowships.

Each of the volume is rich with quarterly Bible lessons, stories, drama, songs, seminar, tract materials and a host of other things that can be used to edify, educate, entertains and evangelize every category of people, ranging from children to elderly persons.

Every volume is designed to equip school teachers, ministers in Churches or campus or office fellowships and other people who wish to work with the Lord.

All These And Other Books Are Distributed Worldwide And Published By The Publishing House Of Calvary Rock Resources

*Ikenne-Remo, Nigeria
*Manchester, United Kingdom
*New York, United States

www.calvaryrock.org